SALINA

Laurent Gaudé

SALINA

THE THREE EXILES

*Translated from the French
by Alison Anderson*

Europa
editions

Europa Editions
1 Penn Plaza, Suite 6282
New York, N.Y. 10019
www.europaeditions.com
info@europaeditions.com

Copyright © 2018 by Actes Sud
First Publication 2021 by Europa Editions

Translation by Alison Anderson
Original title: *Salina. Les trois exiles*
Translation copyright: © 2021 by Europa Editions

Library of Congress Cataloging in Publication Data is available
ISBN 978-1-60945-653-5

Gaudé, Laurent
Salina

Book design by Emanuele Ragnisco
www.mekkanografici.com

Cover image © Kimiko Yoshida

Prepress by Grafica Punto Print – Rome

Printed in the USA

CONTENTS

For my mother,
For my daughter,
From one to the other,
All that passes, lives, and is handed on.

THE DAY OF ORIGINS

At the very beginning of her life, in those days of origins when matter is still unformed, when everything is mere flesh, dull sounds, pulsing, throbbing veins, and breath seeking its way, in those hours when life is not yet certain, when everything can give up and flicker out, there comes that cry, so far away, so strange you might think it is the mountain moaning, weary of its own immobility. The women look up and stay absolutely still, anxious. They hesitate, are not sure they have really heard it, and yet there it comes again: far away, toward the impassable Tadma Mountain, a baby is crying. Are they aware, the women of the Djimba clan, of everything the cry contains? The blood it carries within? The turmoil, the ravaged bodies, the banishing and rage? Do they sense that with that tiny little cry they can hardly identify, something is beginning, something that will not stop growing until it has overturned everything?

Bit by bit the crying becomes sharper. There can be no more doubt: the newborn child is getting closer. Men and women converge toward the village entrance to wait for what is coming. It will take many more long minutes still until a rider appears. He is approaching slowly, vanishes now and again with the twists of the path. He is approaching and he is indeed the source of the child's cries.

Sissoko Djimba, the village chief, calls his warriors. They gather, their muscles tensed, their gaze unflinching. They have no fear. They merely agree that the gods are sending someone to them and they will have to deal with the coming event. They have all put on their ceremonial clothing: long tunics in bright colors, and in their belts, the sword of Takouba, the holy iron of the ancestors. The warm desert wind has risen, causing the village banners to flap and flutter. The men remain absolutely motionless. They know how long it will take for the horseman to reach them, and they wait.

First of all, there is this day of origins, long ago, when after a long wait in the desert heat the horseman arrives at last. He does not vary his speed, does not hesitate or hurry. Now he is a hundred yards from the group. Everyone is trying to identify him, but no one knows the insignia he is wearing. His horse is equipped with leather saddlebags the likes of which no member of the Djimba clan has ever seen. Even at the great market in distant Kamangassa there is no such leatherwork. He must come from farther away than any known land. He is covered in dust. His body moves so little you might think he is glued to his horse, doomed perhaps for months to wander in this way, to go where his mount has decided to take him. How old is he? No one can say. The man moves forward. The Djimbas think for a moment that he will ride through their group without speaking or doing anything, as if their presence were of no importance, but that is not what he does. Ten steps from Sissoko Djimba, he comes to a halt.

Everyone can see clearly now that in his left elbow he is carrying a newborn child in swaddling clothes. And the infant's cries resound. It has not stopped crying. A little creature of flesh has been there for days, weeks, for as far a distance as the strange man has ridden, and it is crying, forcefully, never tiring. It is even a miracle that it has not succumbed to the exhaustion of its tiny body. The silence lasts. Then, slowly, the horseman swings one leg over his horse's rump and steps to the ground. He is still carrying the child. He takes a few steps until he is halfway between Sissoko and his horse and he places the bundle of still shrieking linen onto the ground, then he mounts his horse again, and, without waiting to see what might happen, without saying a word—which in any case he would have uttered in an unknown language that no one could have responded to—unless in the land he hails from there is simply no language—slowly, he rides away again, back to the place he has come from, leaving behind him for the first time in days, perhaps weeks, the cries of the child he has just abandoned.

Among the Djimbas no one moves. The child is on the ground, in the sun, and it is crying. They must wait for Sissoko to make a decision. The child is still crying, filling everything with the presence of its tiny life. The men remain seated. Time passes and Sissoko does not say a word. Everyone understands that he has chosen not to take in the child. They must not risk accepting a child when none of them knows whether it might not bring a curse. Do not act. Do nothing. Stay there until the child wears itself out, drifts into sleep, weakens and dies. The sun is beating down: it won't take long. They are not the ones who will kill it, it is the wind, the sun, the dust. The ones who will kill it are those who brought it into the world and who are no longer there to look after it. The horseman who left it at their feet. But not them. They are merely waiting. Once the infant is dead, they will bury it, respectfully, even carefully, the way they would handle the statue of an unknown, feared divinity. Hours go by. Sweat beads on brows, on the strapped bodies of the warriors. The children sitting by their mothers doze off, struggle to remain upright. Only the infant's cries do not weaken. The cries penetrate every mind, drill into their skulls. The infant is crying with its will to live, its desire to suckle, to satisfy the wrenching of its empty stomach, it is crying from the hot air tearing at its lungs, from the dust in its eyes. The men wait. The sun is at its zenith, strikes the stones with violence, makes them impossible to touch, as if they were slabs of fire. The waiting villagers think it will soon be over but the infant resists and, in the end, it is the sun that yields first. It begins to set, and it is as if the infant has made it bend to its will. Sissoko Djimba is surprised, but he stands tall. If the sun could not manage to overcome this strange living thing there on the ground before them, threatening with all sorts of possible dangers, then the hyenas will. Before long they will come and the men will not move from the sight of their appetite, they will let the beasts pull the bundle toward them, then tear it apart, dismember it, devour it. In the end perhaps there will be no need to dig a grave, there will be nothing but scraps of flesh spread about in a feasting of jaws. What do the gods want, forcing them to witness such carnage?

*

And the hyenas come, with the first flicker of twilight. They announce their presence with long strident cries, like teeth grinding. The cries of the greedy animals cause the infant's cries to stop for a moment. Is it afraid? Does it sense, deep in its small self, that the beasts will sink their fangs into its flesh, dig about in it, tear it open it with their appetite? Its silence does not last. It begins crying again and its cries guide the hyenas, who come closer, warily, and they discover that there by that little bundle of flesh luring them with its weakness and vulnerability there are men, a thick mass of men, an entire village seated there. Fearful of being caught in a trap, but irrepressibly drawn to the flesh on offer, the creatures creep forward, curving their spines like hesitant dogs, fearing the blows they might receive. They whimper with impatience. Finally, when they are six feet from the bundle of linen, when all they need to do is extend their necks and grasp in their fangs the little cries that nothing seems to tire, the hyenas, too, come to a halt. Men and creatures remain facing one another. The infant is still crying. And then Mamambala, fed up, gets to her feet. She asks nothing of Sissoko Djimba, walks through the crowd, and with no fear of the hyenas, which rise on her approach, she grabs hold of the bundle and tucks it into her elbow. The cries cease instantly. Mamambala unfastens her tunic, offers her swollen breast to the infant, and it suckles with a mountainous hunger. She can see that the famished little body is that of a girl, and this makes her smile. And so, she says these words that everyone hears: "For the salt of the tears with which you've covered the earth, I will call you Salina." Only then, as if they had been waiting to hear her name, do the hyenas go away, leaving the little scrap of flesh to the humans to return to their world of dry stones and anxious nights, where decaying carcasses are treasures, and laughter, screams.

I
THE CARAVAN

At the other end of her life, there is this morning, almost the same, when she sits up abruptly on the blanket that serves as her bed. Salina, aged by an entire life of dust, struggle, wandering, and rage. Salina, with her dry, withered body, listening out in the vast landscape. Everything around her is still bathed in a hesitant dawn light that does not dare to banish the night. She concentrates. She cannot say for certain that it really is a cry that woke her. She is not even sure she heard it. For a while, she searches the sky to see whether it is not, rather, a bird of prey, greeting the world the way a sovereign greets his people, but there is nothing . . . At the other end of her life, there is this moment, almost the same, when she is not the one crying, but listening, motionless on that rock that overlooks the landscape all around her, and with her gaze she searches for a confirmation of what she thinks she saw. Does she, in that moment, think that the horseman has come back for her? No. An entire lifetime has gone by, and the horseman was so long ago that he no longer belongs to her memory. Suddenly she hears it again: far away, stifled by the distance. She cannot understand the meaning of it—is it a cry of pain or a celebration of the new day?—but she no longer has any doubt that it is indeed a human noise, sounding at regular intervals in this world of stones. It takes her some time to work out where, in the sleeping landscape, it is coming from. She concentrates her gaze on the land below her, every dune, every contour, and finally she makes out a cloud of dust on the horizon. They are back. There can be no more doubt. A few long minutes go by and again the cry rings out, no longer or shorter than the other times. Out there, a man is telling the daybreak something she cannot hear. So, all of a sudden, she hurries and nervously picks up a goatskin satchel where she has placed a water gourd and some belongings, along with two blankets she now rolls up and ties to her back. Then she takes hold of her walking stick and begins the descent. She knows every stone, does not scrape her feet on any of them. At the other end of her life, there is this morning where she slips urgently along tiny paths of pebbles, despite her age and the wearing of time, and she does so with the confident ease of a goat.

She smiles. She got there before them. Positioned by the side of the path, she waits for the first horsemen in the convoy to appear. She looks for her son, who is there in the column of men and animals, where shapes dissolve into dust. He has been gone for thirty-seven days. Thirty-seven days ago, she entrusted him to the caravan leaders; for thirty-seven days she has been waiting for his return. They left the caravanserai on a day of debilitating heat when the animals' breathing mixed with the men's. They went to sell cattle and pottery for spices and copperware at the great market on the edge of the sand dunes. Today, they have come back and she is afraid. As she is every time. She always dreads this moment. What have the gods decided to do with her son during the long journey she has subjected him to?

As soon as she sees the first horse and rider, she also hears the rider's cry. It has nothing to do anymore with what she heard from the heights of the rock dunes: it is a long, shrill cry that ends in a sort of yelp. She is struck by its power. It is tense, with a veiled intonation that tears at the soul. She knows what it means: the column is bringing back a dead body. One of those who left here thirty-seven days ago is no longer breathing, is nothing but a corpse, fastened to the rear of a dromedary. She freezes, waits, is about to ask the gods why they always take those she loves from her, but she doesn't, she presses her lips together and stands poised. The horseman cries out again. The inhabitants of the oasis emerge now, one after the other, and crowd around her along the road. Everyone is looking closely at the horsemen as they appear. Everyone is searching for the one who is missing. She could die during these moments of waiting; they are like entire lifetimes. And then her son appears at last. Malaka. She recognizes him from the way he carries himself. And so, she lowers her head, leans toward the earth, kisses the palm of her hand, then places it on the ground; repeats the gesture three times in a row, to thank the insatiable gods who, for now, have decided to spare him. No one moves or speaks. No one welcomes the horsemen with cries of joy, the way they customarily do. Only the cry of the herald of death rises from the column. A bit further along, a family stands motionless, stunned, as they come to understand and begin to tremble with the misfortune that has befallen them, a family that only a few minutes earlier was confident and happy, and already they are weeping, feeling severed forever, as they run toward the dromedary to claim the beloved body. But to her nothing else matters, only the fact it was not her son. She shuts herself off from the noise around her. Her gaze follows her son, she sees no one else. She thinks he has changed already—is it possible?—as if the thirty-seven days he has spent away from her have made him a man.

This is the last time she will endure this ordeal. Something deep inside her has decided—not with her mind but with her body, her nerves, the blood pounding in her veins . . . That this is the last time. She will no longer go, the way she has just done, the way she has done dozens of times before, to the gate of the caravanserai, to the head of the column, with her fear of learning that her son is no longer there. For years, her life has been lived to the rhythm of these journeys. Every time the caravan departed, whether it was the dry season, or the time of the great cattle market, she would entrust her son to the column and he would depart, leave the makeshift camp where she lives, take to the roads and get to know the men—and he did all of that without her. Every time, for five years, this has meant for her the ordeal of days spent waiting, her belly twisted in fear, and in all that time there was not one minute when she did not dread that misfortune would suddenly remember her name, Salina, would remember, yes, and decide—why not—to say it again.

The body is carefully taken down. It is restored to its family's arms. A story about the death will be told—accident or combat. There will be questions, stories repeated a thousand times, to respond to the loved ones' inexhaustible thirst, for they will want to know every detail. There will be wakes, to celebrate the man whose life was taken in the dunes, but she will not be there. That will be later, when she is already gone. For now, trade reclaims its rights. The animals must be unloaded. The traders have come a long way, have been waiting for days to inspect the goods and start the transactions. Confusion reigns. The beasts are led to the watering place. They move in a thick herd, raising dust. The women bring little wooden bowls containing camel's milk to the new arrivals. After they have drunk, the men go back to their business and open the big bales of merchandise to display them. She waits slightly to one side because she does not want to bother her son. He has to go on helping them unload. She takes the time to observe him. Something about him has changed: not in his face, or even his body, but in the way the others speak to him. They greet him. Slap him on the shoulder. Young boys his age embrace him. He is one of them, she thinks, and she cannot say whether this real-ization hurts or comforts her. Around her everyone is shouting, calling to one another, bargaining. Bales of cloth are handed back and forth. Bags of spices change hands. This will last two days or more, it makes no dif-ference, they will no longer be there to take part in the commotion of trade. She has already seen too many men for today, had enough of the crowd and the noise, and she is eager to get away, back to the land where she comes from, where the men do not live.

They do not speak, leave behind them the cool air of the oasis, and the tumult of the crowd. She has not yet asked him anything. First of all, they must be in each other's physical presence, and only later will their lips speak. For the time being, they must simply walk side by side, adjusting their gait, rediscovering their silent complicity. They have left the agitation of the market and are going deeper into the mineral silence of the dunes of stone. It feels good to be back in the silence. The sound of men was beginning to make her feel dizzy. Too many voices and bodies, too much bustle and movement bringing too many memories of vindictive crowds, shouts, insults.

Once again, it is just the two of them on the vast land, mother and son, living at the same rhythm, walking at the same pace, cautiously keeping their distance from the company of men. The young man is filled with happiness to be in the dense air. He feels as if he has found the silence from which he was born. The days are vast and need no words. They are at home in inhospitable deserts of stone that imprison the heat and amplify sound. She has told him how to make shrubbery into a camp. She has taught him the course of the springs, the water running beneath the dunes. They know how to decipher the intentions of the sky and the anger of the wind. Life is made of gathering, hunting for small prey, hours spent counting the stars or listening to her stories. Today, he has found his mother's stone face again, her stubborn way of walking, and it seems to him that something in this landscape of pebbles is immutable.

Everything is there, absolutely the same. Again, he sees his mother's shelter built against the desert mountain. It is a wall of stones built in a circle, covered with a roof of dried palm leaves and dead branches. Again, he finds the little wooden structure, not far from the hut, rooted to the ground with heavy stones: long wooden poles planted in the earth and covered with a sort of roof where they can place all sorts of things—water gourds, provisions, utensils—to ensure they are out of reach of the rodents. Further along, he rediscovers the pen where Salina takes her goats for the night. It is the realm of flies, which circle in a thick perfume of musk.

Salina builds a fire. He waits for her to speak the way she always does. He is eager. It has always been like this. In the evening, when she has washed the copper plates by rubbing them in the sand, she speaks. And the young man has always filled himself with her words, avidly, sensing that they have been given to him so that he can grow up. All these stories. All these tales. This, more than anything else, is what she has given him, every time they have sat by the fire. A thousand times, she has told him strange sagas, of battles and barbarian myths, a thousand times, her past and the brutal era in which she was born. He listened to everything, avidly, amazed that this woman could contain so many words. Amazed that his mother, who lived for nothing else other than these long days spent by his side, days of walking, camping, survival, could have had a life so full of pain and upheaval. He sometimes thought she was making it up, but the feeling quickly disappeared. Sometimes there was a choking in her voice that could not lie, something inside her breaking, she would stumble over the same name, or always wipe her eyes when evoking the same scene. He wants to hear her repeat the details he already knows, wants to hear the same stories again, but she won't oblige him. After a while, she looks up and says, "Today it's your turn to speak . . . " His turn to say what he has seen and experienced. His turn to tell her about the spice market in the north, and the death of the young man. His turn to explain life in the column, day after day, and the languages he has learned. At first, Malaka hesitates, but his eyes are shining. He is by the fire, he finishes eating the dried dates she has handed to him, and he talks about his thirty-seven days on the road. The more he speaks, the more she can sense his joy, his young man's excitement. And what his voice tells her is not about the confused bivouacs of the column, which were intoxicating moments to him, nor the thrill of being part of such a big caravan, what his voice tells her, beyond the story he makes of it, is that life has gone by. Her son is there before her, as tall as a man. She looks at him with emotion, as if she were seeing him for the first time. Their eyes meet, but he does not understand that this is the gaze of a mother who has discovered that her child no longer really belongs to her. She lets him speak, hoping he will go on all night long, even if she falls asleep, even if the fire goes out and the night chill descends upon them: let him speak and tell her everything he has seen, so that these moments will last and last and never end. She was right to entrust him to the column. When he was still a newborn baby, she had sworn she would. In spite of her fear and her maternal reticence, she had sworn she would tear him from her arms, often. It is what she has always called "the oath of Alika." Now she feels he does not need to travel anymore. He is ready. He knows what he must know. And so, when he has stopped speaking, when the night has fallen and the goats have gathered, huddling together in anticipation of the chill that will come down from the mountains, she looks at him and says simply, "Tomorrow we will leave." She says it in a voice that is clear of doubt. There is no need to specify either where or why. He understands that what they are going to leave tomorrow is not only this land of rock and pebble, the surrounding mountains, and this old hut filled with the years of the objects of exile, but also their very life as they know it.

II
FAR FROM MANKIND

S he has taken two goats and left the pen open behind her. The other two animals came out and disappeared into the labyrinth of rocks around them. She has taken the copper utensils she needs but was careful not to pack too heavy a load. Malaka looks one last time at the encampment, sensing that he won't be coming back. Salina lived here, he thinks, his gaze lingering on his mother's little shelter. Salina lived here and now she is going away, leaving behind this jumble of a life, this collection of branches and stones that, from now on, will harbor nothing but the wind. He gazes at it all and is surprised to realize he feels no sadness at their departure. The rest is waiting for him, and it is vaster, more intoxicating. So, he runs to catch up with his mother, for she has already disappeared behind the crest heading east, and his joy is that of a child.

They walk one behind the other, saving their strength in this desert of dust that defeats even the birds. This is not the first time they have gone away. Salina has built several encampments here and there, always far from the villages, always half hidden by the rock. But until now, their wandering obeyed the order of the seasons: they came and went from one place to another depending on the time of year. Now they are leaving, and that's different. The days follow one another. He wonders if she knows where they are going or whether she has just decided to go as far east as possible. There is no more storytelling in the evening. When the sun sets, she maintains a focused silence. He doesn't dare ask anything. He looks at the great Mount Tadma coming closer on the horizon. He wonders if that is where they're going. Mount Tadma, which he has never climbed, and beyond which no one has ventured. Only once did he go with the column of caravanners to the cloth trading post. It's a little village to the south, at the foot of the mountain range. The last inhabited place before the summits. At the beginning of the dry season, when the snows have melted, there is trading there with people from the other world, who cross the mountain on paths that they alone know, and who come to sell their cloth with its colors the likes of which no one has ever seen. He liked the trading post and stayed there several months, the time it took to learn the language of those dark-skinned men, who were masters of the forges because, they said, they controlled the stream water. The cloth trading post was the only point of contact between these two worlds, so far apart. No caravans had ever ventured any further. Mount Tadma, for them, was the edge of the known world. And yet, it is toward Mount Tadma that they are walking now. Not along the path that leads to the trading post, but heading much farther north, straight into the barrier of mountains, as if it might open the moment they draw near.

Sometimes she stumbles and that is new. She has moments of dizziness that she tries to hide, but he notices.

It's as if the ground is playing with her. For a fraction of a second, it gives way under her. And then she must reach out for his arm. She calls him by his name, breathing rapidly, "Malaka . . . " He is proud to feel that she needs him. It lasts only a few seconds: very quickly, the world rights itself and Salina continues walking. Very quickly, she is tireless again.

One day, they come at last to the top of a hill and Malaka stands there gaping. Opposite him is Mount Tadma, solid and majestic. He has never seen it so close. It looks like a fortress covered with snow. The air has changed: a cold wind is hurtling down the slopes of the mountain, icing their skin and stinging their eyes. But all of a sudden, while he is immersed in this vision, Salina falters. He hears her body fall, her head striking a root with a dull thud. He rushes over, cries her name, repeats it, "Salina!" until she opens her eyes, at first with difficulty, and then more confidently, smiling when she sees her son's face. He is relieved she has come around. He helps her sit up, props her against a tree, offers her some water. She drinks in silence, her gestures slow. Then, lifting her face to him, with an almost childlike smile, half-sorry, half-cheerful, she murmurs, "I think I have begun to die." He is stunned, wants to cry out, "No!", to pick her up, convince her of her strength, but he knows she is telling the truth. He can sense it. Suddenly, he understands why they went away, why they have been walking eastward since their departure. Salina is dying and she wants to find a land in which to rest.

Now he carries her. Her strength is abandoning her,

and she can no longer walk. Her body has become so light that it is not a weight, or hardly . . . Sometimes, he can feel her hand squeezing his shoulder. It is not to ask him to stop, it is just to make sure he is there, alive beneath her, vigorous. Sometimes, she falls asleep. And then he feels her body grow heavier. Her arms slip down along her sides and dangle in the void. He has to be careful then, not to let her fall backwards.

He hesitated for a moment when he was about to begin climbing Mount Tadma. He had to resign himself to abandoning the two goats, which had become too great a burden. He hesitated because the mountain seemed too high, climbing it too ambitious. She must have sensed this. She put a gentle pressure on his shoulder to encourage him, to confirm that this was indeed where he had to go, and that no fear must slow their progress. And so, he continued walking.

They climb patiently and carefully, seeking out the path across the flank of the mountain, sometimes stopping until the wind dies down. They set up camp at the foot of a tree when they find one, or in the shelter of a boulder. Every day a new departure. Every day continuing their ascent. Even if they go only a few hundred yards. Gradually, the vegetation disappears, trees become rare, grass gives way to rocky ground. There are scarcely any birds, and the air tastes more and more like frost. They must walk. On and on. That is what she is saying with the little pressing movements of her hands. He obeys. Without knowing whether he will find a path through the increasingly hostile landscape. Everything is becoming narrower and steeper. Sometimes, he has to scramble up the rocks. Then he prays is that she is holding fast to him and will not let go. He is overcome by dizziness in those moments when everything depends on the strength she still has, or not, to cling to him. She holds on. Does not let go. And they climb together, in spite of the fatigue, they climb up to the first snows.

They are far from everything now. The world of people is behind them. They are above the clouds. His mother is like an extension of himself, on his back. He has become so used to her weight, to her faint breathing, that he no longer notices. As so, he is startled when one day she speaks again. She has not spoken in so long. "I will not know the place of my death . . . " she says. He is about to stop. He wants to look for a flat boulder where he can set her down and try to give her something to drink, or feed her a few berries, but he feels the pressure of her hand on his shoulder and he knows this means he must go on. Later—how much time has gone by?—she speaks again, and her voice rings clear, astonishingly soft, in this stony world creaking with the wind. "You will carry me there." He doesn't answer. He concentrates, to keep going on without stumbling or falling. The wind is blowing harder, lifting the snow at the edge of the path, enclosing them in a whirlwind that whips their faces. Have two bodies ever been more tightly bound, their breathing more attuned? His steps are slow. Everything is creaking and whistling. They are wrapped in animal skins that are stiff with the biting frost. Whenever he moves, the scarf he has wrapped around his neck hurts his chin, bites into his skin. The mountain seems to want to close around them. The wind whistles into the gorges and makes their ears hum. It is lashing them, freezing them, but Malaka resists. And slowly, with each passing day, the light returns.

One morning, the wind drops. He does not know whether it is his fingers or his face that feel greater relief. The path they are following gets progressively wider. They have gone over a mountain pass. He continues a bit further. As far as a huge stone ledge that overlooks the void. From there, for the first time, he can see the other face of the world, immense, unfolding before his eyes with the slowness of becalmed days. Everything is greener, lusher, and the distance reaches on and on to a vastness of water he has never seen. He is about to put Salina down, to tell her that the hardest is behind them, that from now on they will only have to go down, but he doesn't. He stands there motionless, his mother clinging to his back. He lets himself be filled by the silence around them. She has died. He knows this. He can no longer feel her breathing against his neck. Her arms and legs have gone rigid, as if she wanted to be sure not to fall, even in death. He is alone, for the first time, with his lifeless mother on his back. She will not see that land stretching so calmly before them. She will not marvel at the ocean on the horizon, or all the things he is about to discover: the new sounds, the luxuriant trees. She will know nothing of those lands he will explore, but she is there, still, close to him, and now he must find a place to bury her in this new immensity.

III
THE CEMETERY ISLAND

The son's long preparation of his mother's body begins. He has mixed sap from a tree with water from a stream. He has perfumed his mixture with strong, fragrant herbs. Everything is ready. He hesitates for a moment beside his mother's body. Her nakedness troubles him: her breasts loose like emptied pockets, the sparse hairs of her pubis, the soft flesh of her thighs, her hair uncovered . . . He has so rarely seen her hair like that. Salina always wore her dark blue veil, which protected her from the wind and the sand. Still, he doesn't move, wonders how he will manage. He must force himself, go beyond his unease. The body before his eyes is no longer modest. It is dead. She is naked, like trees, like rocks. He will pass his hand over her and it will be like passing his hand over a mound of humus or down the bark of a tree. But still he hesitates until, at last, he takes the old woman's fingers in his hand, and using a cloth, as carefully as a nurse, he moistens them one after the other with the balm he has created.

He takes his time. Memories of the past emerge with each finger. He feels them, lets them escape, to float on the air for a while then vanish. Each finger tells a story and allows what she was to depart. Each finger and then both arms, with the same slowness. The son slowly preparing his mother. It takes hours. He feels everything, and when night has fallen, he stops, conscious that he must not hurry. The next day, he continues. And the day after that. He goes on, raises her head, takes even more time for her face. He must be painstaking. Her mouth, with all the words she uttered, hissed, all the words that never came out, that she could not express, and which died with her like little unborn things. And then it is time for her lips—a whole day to close them gently, so they will not be frozen in a grimace of pain or boredom, but a faint smile, a gentle, calm curve. The son runs his hands one last time over the dead woman. Running over her body, day after day, right to the legs which walked so far. An entire life doing nothing else, from birth to death. Roads, paths of stone or sand, dry lands, lands of exile. His hands run over her belly, even her genitals. It all comes back to him. He closes his eyes, lets these odors of life vibrate inside him, these sensations of the past buried in the flesh, and which the flesh is releasing as it dissolves. It is all there. In this body as it shrivels and lets its memory escape one last time.

Every evening, when he has finished embalming part of the body, when he has delicately set down whatever he has just covered with unguent, every evening he goes into the forests and screams. He has to bite into life, feel it, shout it out loud if he does not want to be in danger of remaining on the side of the dead. He strikes tree trunks, runs headlong down the slope, mindless of where he is going or whether he will find his way again. Nothing matters. He is a body in full flight, dance, outpouring, exhaustion. Every night, after the painstaking calm of the son preparing his mother, he rolls upon himself in the woods and shouts so loudly that the animals flee. He weeps, screams, foams at the mouth. He arches his back, dances every night unto exhaustion.

Walk. Find this vertigo of being in the world without existing for anyone anymore. His mother is no longer there pressing her hand on his shoulder, showing him the way with the obstinacy of a compass. Everything is slow, everything seizes hold of him, slows him. He has built a stretcher for Salina's body. He has stopped speaking. Who would he speak to? He is alone in a world that knows nothing of him. And he tries to recall her voice, Salina's voice, her broken voice that so often told him those stories of the origins, which so often carried its tales of struggle and war, her voice wrapping around him on starry nights when there were just the two of them, her voice that has now left the world, like a tide weary of the sand.

In the valley, the ground is covered with grass and it is easier to pull the stretcher now. The earth is rich, gorged on water. Before long, he comes to a river and decides to continue along it. This is where the first men appear. At first, he is afraid of them, but then changes his mind when he realizes how calmly they accept his presence. In the expanses of tall grass, peasants are digging, working the land; sometimes they look up without straightening their backs and stare with surprise at this man whom no one knows and who is passing by, but they ask no questions. They wipe their brows, sometimes make a slow gesture with their hands, and Malaka does not know whether it is to protect their eyes from the sun or to greet him. He also sees women, at the bend in the river, leaning over the water to do the washing or bathe their children, and they stop singing or arguing when they see him go by. No one asks him anything. They are not surprised by his presence. He is a traveler, or a god, it hardly matters. It is not up to them to decide.

The tall grasses gradually become sparser and now there is even a path by the riverbank. He follows it, walks without knowing where he is going until one day, in the distance, ramparts are visible. He pauses for a moment. He has never seen such a thing: low, wide walls that look like a fold in the earth. He goes nearer. The entire length of the wall is covered with frescoes crowded with men, women, plants, and animals of all kinds, all together, depicting attacks, wars, loving embraces. An entire nation has been sculpted. Or are they real men and women, immobilized in stone, expiating some sin they have committed and waiting for the day when they will be able to return to life, to break free and scatter throughout the town . . . For a moment, he hesitates, does not know whether he ought to continue and go closer. All around him, the crowd is growing thicker. By the great gate to the city, a column of men and women are entering the walled town, while others are coming out. They bump against each other, jostle. Voices, bodies, wicker baskets, the smells of a market, animals, all colliding together and paying no attention to his presence, never asking him what he is carrying on his stretcher. And so, he joins the crowd, amid the shouts and calls, and passes in turn through the great gate.

Caught in the maze of little streets, he makes his way as best he can, lets the crowd carry him. The streets draw him in, impose their rhythm. After a while, the crowd thins somewhat and, at last, he can walk more slowly. His head is buzzing. He sees nothing but poverty before him and it jars with the elegance of the walls he left behind at the gate—as if only the city were rich, whereas its inhabitants are condemned to nakedness and dirt. On the squares he crosses, he sees twisted, crippled bodies limping through the mud. Emaciated women, at their wits' end as greedy infants suckle them, look up as he goes by, then away again. He sees senile old people rolling their eyes like lunatics and inserting prayers, in a furtive voice, into the cracks in the facades. Oh, the city too full of the living, the city grown haggard on itself, full, too full, of hunger and exhaustion. Following the alleyways at random, he eventually finds himself by a canal. All along the water, boats are moored, tied to one another. Mountains of vegetables or piles of cloth, everything is for sale. The canal is filthy. He sees bodies floating in the water and no one seems to care, as if those dead bodies belonged to no one. They rock gently in the lapping water and glide slowly toward the estuary, like indolent dolls, nibbled at by fish. He continues to walk along the quays, crosses squares packed with vendors and swarms of children who call out to him. He lets the city lead him astray, and eventually ends up on a huge square. All at once, everything opens out onto the sea, immense and dazzling. He is amazed. He did not think the sea was so near. The gray paving on the square extends before him in a sparkling expanse, and the sea air makes him giddy.

A man is watching him. Sitting on the quayside, leaning on a long wooden stick. He is surrounded by little monkeys. Some of them are asleep between his legs, others climb up and down his motionless body, calmly, occasionally nestling on his head or in his hair. Without really knowing why, Malaka goes up to the man and nods. He hesitates, then says the word "cemetery," in a questioning voice. At first, the old man does not reply, then, very slowly, almost without moving, making only those gestures that are absolutely necessary, he points in the direction behind his back. Malaka looks out, seeking what the man might be pointing to, but there is nothing but the sea. Is the man suggesting that he should let Salina slip into the water? Then suddenly his gaze catches on a shape on the horizon. An island. So, he asks his question again, pointing to the island, "Cemetery?" The man nods. What Malaka does not see is that all around them something has changed. Conversations have broken off. People are looking at him. What Malaka doesn't hear is the word all the curious onlookers are whispering, "Darzagar . . . Darzagar"—the old man's name. All across the square, people have stopped what they were doing, have fallen silent, are observing them. Little by little, he realizes that it is because he spoke to this man, but he doesn't know whether he has committed a sin or, rather, is addressing a holy personage. Suddenly, Darzagar's voice rings out, calmly. He looks straight at Malaka with his gray-green eyes and says, "Where are you from?"

"From beyond the mountain."

"Which mountain?"

"The one we call Tadma, which separates the worlds."

"Who have you brought with you?"

"My mother."

All around them, the square has stopped moving. Only cats still slink along the walls in search of some meager pittance. Darzagar sits up straight, leaning on his long wooden stick. The little monkeys that had settled on his shoulders, neck, or lap slide one after the other along his clothing and frolic at his feet, surprised that they have had to move, sorry to leave this human warmth behind. The man has the deliberate gestures of a mountain. He carefully pushes off the last little mammals, then, with the help of his stick, gets to his feet, stretching to his full height. He is thin, bare-chested, his belly almost entirely covered by his beard.

"The boat is waiting for you," he says, pointing to a small craft that looks as if it has been anchored there since the city became a city.

The dhow weaves its way through the traders' boats, clumps of seaweed, and tangles of branches. The old man presses against his stick, his movements are sure, he never makes more effort than is required. On the square they have left behind, men and women have crowded to the edge of the quay and are watching in silence as they draw away. Whenever they pass another boat, faces turn toward them, shouts cease, conversations come to a sudden halt. All eyes follow them. And, as if he has understood that Malaka is wondering why the crowd is gazing at them in surprise, the tall old man, between two thrusts of his oar, explains, "I have been waiting for this day for so long. And all the city has, too . . . "

Without really knowing what it means, Malaka understands that the astonishment he can read on the faces of those they pass is due to this: the honor—but is it an honor?—of being on this boat, of seeing the old man once again bent over his long wooden stick, ferrying the person he has taken on board out to sea.

They leave the land behind. Malaka lets himself go to the rocking motion. At first, he was afraid, but now he is enthralled and totally absorbed by the bright glinting of light on the water. Eventually, he asks whether the island they can see is indeed the cemetery, and Darzagar answers that it is not. In the bay, there are five islands in a row, like a string of pearls. The cemetery island is the last one. The way will be long.

"Will I be able to bury my mother there?" asks Malaka.

"The cemetery will decide," answers the ferryman.

Then he gives another great push, letting the boat glide forward, and he explains that the cemetery where he is taking Malaka is sacred. The island is enclosed by a wall. There is only one gate, a thick one, that no man can open. The dead are taken on board, and for the entire duration of the crossing, the life story of the deceased must be told. The cemetery hears the story. And at the end of the journey, it will decide if the gate must open or not. The old man tells of entire families who have been ferried across and presented themselves to the wall: there are those who tell so little because they discover they know nothing, there are those who do not agree and argue along the way, there are those who lie, who embellish . . . He tells Malaka how the gate to the cemetery has been closed for so long. Is it because the cemetery is full that it refuses to open? Is it to punish the inhabitants for a crime they might have committed without even noticing? No one knows. But the gate remains locked.

Once the old man has finished, he plunges his stick into the water and pushes with all his strength, then says, "Once we have left the bay, you will be able to begin the story of the woman you have brought with you."

Malaka does not reply, suddenly trying to gather all his memories, all the stories Salina told him in her lifetime. He thinks back to all those images that overwhelmed him while, as the son, he was preparing his mother, but they had come to him out of order, in fragments. He thinks back to the stories she herself told about her childhood in the desert encampments. And for the first time, he tries to envision Salina's life as a story he would have to tell.

Once they are on the open ocean, waves appear. They are not strong, but it is a new rolling motion that Malaka is not used to. He grips the side of the boat, his hands clenched. The sunlight fades in intensity. The islands remain invisible. He can only see the first one. The others are hidden by a sort of mist that makes the horizon uncertain. He feels ready. He has thought about where to begin his story. He is about to speak when Darzagar raises his hand to stop him, "Not yet. We have to wait for the boat of witnesses."

And he pulls his long stick out of the water, places it in the bottom of the boat, and ceases all activity so that their boat will stop moving. They are too far from the coast now for the pole to be of any use. Darzagar sits in the prow, facing Malaka, and does not speak. He has settled down to wait and Malaka can tell that this might last for hours. But that is not what matters anymore. The boat is slowly drifting, as if the old ferryman had entrusted it to the sea, or the moon, or some other power that Malaka does not know, but which governs the order of things. The world must make a decision and they can neither hurry nor influence it.

At last it comes, the boat Darzagar has been waiting for. It has a reddish-brown sail. It is a fisherman who followed them, just when they left the quay. When the boat comes closer, Malaka can see numerous woven baskets filled with fruit, weighing down the boat. The fisherman slows down and then, without saying a word, without asking a thing, brings his boat alongside Darzagar's. His entire family is with him: a black-eyed woman, and children all around. How many are there? Four? Five? Malaka can see only sleeping legs, arms curled around other arms, nestled in colored blankets that must smell of brine. The two boats are now closely joined. The trader has not lowered his sail. He goes back to the tiller. He will steer both boats. No one has spoken. There are no introductions, but Darzagar slowly stands up, and with a piece of chalk, he draws a strange sign on the wood of the other boat. He utters a sentence Malaka does not understand, then turns to him and says, "Through this sign on the boat, languages mingle, and all words will be understood."

Then he sits back down and in a calm voice, looking Malaka straight in the eye, he says, "Now you may begin."

Malaka knows it is time to tell who his mother was. He knows it is time to say the old name of Salina, which now exists only for him, and which he has kept like a precious belonging. And it is as if, all of a sudden, another world has suddenly burst into the soft evening, a dry, arid world, made of blood, of wounds, and filled with the pungent odor of hyenas.

IV
FIRST BLOOD

I, Malaka, son raised in the desert by a mother who spoke to stones, will tell you of Salina, the woman of three exiles. I will tell of my mother, who is lying here at the bottom of the boat, and the world that will appear will be one of dust and cries. In the time when the world greeted her life, there were suns that caused skin to bleed, and a savage desire for vengeance. In the time when the world greeted her life, there was a child who had come out of nowhere. Salina was born far away, so far that no one knows the exact place, nor whose child she was, even she did not know. I, Malaka, who must tell the story of her life in order for the cemetery to decide whether to open its gate or not, I have chosen to begin with that day of walking, at the other end of her life, for that is where everything begins. A day of scorching heat when an entire village turned to look toward the mountains. I have known them for a long time, the words I shall say. I did not know the rough days of combat. My mother told me about them, but she did not remember them, either. She knew them from another voice, the voice of Mamambala. She is the one who told her what I am going to say. I, Malaka, the son of a long chain of voices, am picking up the stories from before my lifetime, handed down from mouth to mouth, from one campfire to another, and I will bring to you what that day was. Do not trust my solitude, there are many of us in this boat: an entire world is there before you through my voice."

Malaka falls silent for a moment to catch his breath. No one moves. All eyes are on him. In that instant, he knows he will have the strength to speak for a long time. He feels good. It is as if time were suspended. Nothing comes to shatter the intensity of the night. And so, he begins his story. He talks about the hyenas, about that day when minutes were long, and the sun eventually yielded. He talks about the man who appeared out of nowhere, who did not say a word. He explains the uninterrupted cries of the newborn child. He describes the face-to-face encounter between the men and the hyenas, with the infant in the middle, and he says that on that day, it was the animals that yielded. He tells of Mamambala and her comforting voice. The woman standing before the clan, breaking the order of immobility and naming the child. He tells of the drought and the riddle of that long-ago day that is like a birth, then he falls silent, astonished that he has spoken so much. All during his tale, Darzagar has not moved. The boat has slowly drifted forward, carried by the wind. The ferryman has stayed upright, motionless, completely absorbed in listening. The fisherman's wife has come closer, too. She is sitting upright against their boat to be sure not to miss any of the story, holding one child in her arms and patting it on the shoulder to lull it; another one nestled in her legs. The two boats continue to move forward in the night, slowly, neither hesitant nor hurried. No one breaks the silence. Malaka thinks again of everything he has just said, all those words that left his lips. He didn't make anything up. Everything he said had been told to him, but he has become its agent, and this is the first time he has done so. The story he is narrating takes him back to that woman and he finds himself thinking that, deep down, he does not know her.

"I, Malaka," he continues, "the son of long waking nights in the desert, I will say this before you: I do not know who the child was. I have often thought about it. When I was young, at the markets in the caravanserais, I heard them speak of 'bad luck children.' In the kingdom of lakes, it would seem they have a tradition to appease the greed of ill fate: they choose ten children from the clan and lose them. They do not kill them, they are sent out into the world, each one accompanied by a man who has been instructed to abandon them as far away as possible. The ten children are taken from their families. The day of the separation, everything is weeping and moaning, mothers are frantic, there are cries of revolt, but the ten warriors are chosen for their toughness. They must come back empty-handed. They leave the chosen infants on the routes of the world. Some of them die—of hunger, or exhaustion, or because they are taken in by people who neglect them or are wary of them. Others survive, adopted where they have been abandoned. Through this gesture, the people of the lakes scatter what is potential, and assuage the ill humor of fate, grown irritable with too much opulence, too much peace, demanding its pound of flesh. Was Salina one of those children, offered to the roads to appease misfortune? I don't know . . . unless she was the punishment of that man we will never know anything about, other than his face of dust. Was he condemned to take on a child that cried day and night? What sin did he commit? What I know and what I can say is that one day, for some unknown reason, obeying an obscure rule, the man sensed that, outside the village of the Djimbas, the time of his punishment or of his mission was coming to its end, and that he would be released from the cries that for weeks had been drilling into his brain. From that day forward, Salina became a child. She emerged from the indistinct matter that could have swallowed her at any moment: the dust of the desert, the jaws of the hyenas. She got away from the smells of sweat of man and beast, and Mamambala's arms brought her into the world. What I am going to tell now, is what my mother remembered. She told me the story herself. It is no longer a scene lost in the past, but a constellation of memories, and it is as if I am putting my steps in hers."

Malaka thinks of all this and knows he will never have an answer, that he will never be able to say, with certainty, who his mother was, and what the weeping of the origins contained. But he knows that the words he has just said are those that she herself conveyed to him and which she had received from Mamambala. This woman he never knew appears abruptly in the night, almost takes form, since it is her words that are spoken. He will take up the thread of his narration and he knows that, henceforth, it is Salina's voice he will hear. She told him the story so often. At a certain word, her voice always broke. On evoking a certain man, her eyes would stare at the fire with hatred. He looks at the canvas bag at his feet, protecting her remains from the spray of the ocean. Rage rose so often in her voice, whenever she related the insults they had thrown in her face, the abuse they made her suffer.

He is about to continue when, all of a sudden, Darzagar turns his head. They had been so still that now the movement surprises Malaka, and he also turns his head. To his left, slightly behind them, a new boat has appeared. One of the men on board is slowly waving a large lantern. The fisherman accompanying them slows down, maneuvers in such a way as to offer the newcomers the other side, and, once again, the boats are lashed together. Darzagar's dhow is flanked on either side by fishing boats. During the entire maneuver, no one speaks, no one explains anything. The operation takes place in silence. Ropes are tossed, gestures are quick. And when at last they have finished, they all sit on the wooden benches in their boats, their faces turned to Malaka, and he knows he can continue.

"I, Malaka, son of the riddle, cannot tell an entire childhood: those long days of silence when Salina is no more than a body huddled against Mamambala's. Then her progress, her hesitation, her attempts . . . the days of trying something new, babbling, walking, then speaking. I cannot tell the months that go by, the years, and yet I should, because that is when she becomes a member of the village. That is when she strides across her land and comes to know every corner of every hut. I should, because that is when she is happy. A child who is running, playing, with nothing else before her but a succession of ever-renewed days of freedom. And so, I will say that the infant becomes a child. That the puny body of the little thing that was laid down before the hyenas becomes strong and vigorous. Mamambala watches out for her. She breast-feeds her. Salina grows, walks, listens, questions her. Mamambala teaches her everything: the play of stones in the bed of streams, the sound of the seasons, the way a girl's hair can be arranged according to the colors of the sky. She prays to the spirits with her, at her side. Her smell in their bed, generous and rich, is that of kindness. I cannot tell all those years and yet I should, for that is when she meets Kano, the son of Sissoko Djimba. For her, he is a little boy she plays with, discovers the world with. Kano, whom she loves. From the beginning. For as long as she can remember, because he is both the other and herself. With him there are races, games, their first fears, and their vows, lifelong. With him, the thousand things that are nothing, the thousand innocuous, happy gestures of childish love and the certainty that life is there—safe, full, and luminous. I cannot tell the details of every day, the trust that grows between the woman and the little girl, but I do know this: there is only one thing Mamambala did not say, and that was that growing up is an exile."

Salina changes, becomes a little girl, grows in height and beauty. She grows and does not know that there is a day that will come, a day that will prove them right, all those who laughed whenever she said she would never get married. She does not know that there is this day that will come when the world will seize her by her hair and take possession of who she is. Sissoko Djimba, the village chief, has two sons: Saro and Kano. Saro is the eldest. He is already a young warrior. He is eager to test his mettle. Salina does not see that Saro has already started to hover around her. He acts like an animal that knows it must be patient. He is always there, lurking, following her everywhere, popping out of the foliage, laughing from the other bank of the river, or remaining motionless like a sentinel at the top of the dune while she carries water to the village. From the day of her arrival, Saro has been watching over her like an owner jealously guarding his livestock. She doesn't care. She plays with Kano, is intoxicated with him. Kano and his brown curls, his smile of a gazelle, agile Kano, her accomplice, who is the entire world to her. Often, when she grows annoyed with Saro's presence, she rushes over to him and asks defiantly, "And what do you think you want?" And he never replies, or answers with phrases that are so strange they make her smile. "It will come," he says, before leaving. Spitting on the ground is not enough. Running away is not enough. "One day you will be mine," he says. Answering, "Never!" is not enough. Shouting that she loves only Kano, that if she has to belong to someone it will be Kano, is not enough. Saro grows cold as stone. His lips pursed, his gaze hard, he goes up to her—standing so close that she can smell his male odor, and it bewitches and disgusts her at the same time—and says that, if he wanted to, he could take her right then and there, whenever he feels like it, that no one will stop him because he is the eldest Djimba and that is enough. He is the son of Sissoko and all he has to do is look at something for it to belong to him—and he has looked at Salina. He says that if he doesn't throw himself at her right then and there, it is because he isn't stupid. It would be absurd to taste a fruit that is not yet ripe when you can wait until it is. When she hears this, she always rolls her eyes in anger and runs off, but what he says frightens her. More than the actual words, which she does not fully understand, what she fears is his self-confidence. But

Kano always ends up reassuring her. He goes and finds her and banishes the pout from her face; he leads her away and their games resume.

And then there is that day, as long as a dying sun, there is that day by the stream when she is alone, when she has gone to do the washing so that Mamambala won't have to. The flies are buzzing around more noisily than usual, as stubborn as cloying perfume. There is that day when she feels heavy, slow. As if everything around her were sticking to her fingers. As if the air had decided to stop moving. Washing laundry is hard work. Her back is aching. There is that day when she stands up and suddenly lets out a cry: blood is running down her thighs. Thick. Viscous. Between her thighs, her genitals are swollen. She does not understand. The stream is polluted. She steps back, ashamed by the trace she has left in the water. She inhales, short of breath, takes a few more steps back. The blood is dripping onto the vegetation, onto the sand. She is ashamed, as if she were soiling everything she touched. She is obsessed by the sight of this blood coming from her body. She can feel no pain, but it seems to her that she is losing something. Her eyes are riveted to these traces, and she does not pay attention to the greed of the world around her. She thinks only of Mamambala. She wishes she were there, by her side, she wants to squeeze her hand, ask her what is happening, hear her advice, and follow it to the letter so that this thing will stop as soon as possible and everything will be normal again. She wants her kindly smile, her smell of old earth. And it is only when Saro's shout rings out that she realizes she is not alone, that he has been spying on her and that he knows what her stain is. It is a powerful laugh, a laugh full of triumph and excitement. She understands that Saro is glad, because this blood she has lost—somehow or other—is what he has been waiting for whenever he was watching her. The threat seems so great to her that when Mamambala comes running, slow and burdened by her own weight, her eyes frantic, all Salina can say, a weak defense against Saro's laughter, are these words, over and over, "I don't want to . . . I don't want to . . . "

From that day on, Saro comes even more often than before. He hovers around the shack where Mamambala has hidden Salina. He comes to smell her, to sniff her. Sometimes, when Mamambala is not there, he steals in, to make her cry out in fear and anger, and he goes so close that his face almost touches hers, then he licks her and runs away. She feels imprisoned, stiff. Her swollen breasts are painful. Her head is heavy. She hates this new stickiness between her legs because she understands that nothing but tears will come of it. She stands there, exhausted and unhappy, and the days are long. "How much longer, Mamambala?" she asks, exhausted. And the old woman says nothing, makes a knowing grimace, and prepares her a fortifying juice from roots. How many more slow days when she feels like an insect caught in a spider's web? She thinks the world has stopped. "Do women all bleed at the same time, Mamambala?" The old woman still doesn't speak. She places a cloth soaked in water on the girl's neck to cool her. "Where does all the blood go? And why do the boys seem happy about it?" Mamambala rummages around, tidies, offers her some more to drink, but doesn't answer. "When will the world start again?" If

Mamambala answered, she would say that the world was still rushing along. Salina thought it had stopped the way she had, but outside everything is busy. Saro has not wasted his time. He has been coming and going, he has already spoken to Khaya, his mother, and to Sissoko, from whom he obtained a nod of the head, which means consent. The world has never stopped, the world is busy. And when Saro appears, sticking his head through the canvas flap of the shack, or making excited little cries as he circles around it, old Mamambala knows there is nothing she can do, and sighs. "What is this wound that makes us bleed, Mamambala?" asks Salina. The old woman would have liked to tell her how childhood leaves us at a certain moment, about the freedom that young girls lose with their first blood, but she says nothing, leaves Salina in silence, while in the village, preparations have already begun. And when at last the blood stops flowing, and Salina again feels joyful and light and comes out of the shack eager to find Kano, to run with him, after all this time they have lost, she stands stock-still. Something outside has changed. On the other huts in the village, the women have hung festive bunting. Salina looks and hesitates. She is afraid of what is coming. She turns to Mamambala and says, "What's happening?" The old woman wishes she could say nothing, but she cannot. Salina is already repeating her question: "Mamambala? What does it all mean?" And the words she hears are those she has been dreading: "Your wedding day has been announced."

V
THE WEDDING OF THE BATTLEFIELD

Salina knows that the Djimbas will not go back on their decision, that she does not have that power, but she has another idea. She runs through the village streets. She goes straight to the royal hut. When she stops outside, neither making herself known, nor waiting to find out whether Khaya Djimba will receive her, she enters the hut and goes down on one knee. Then, with her head down, not looking up, she begins to speak. She tells Khaya that she has learned she is to be married. She says she will not oppose it. She is short of breath. She tries to remain calm. She continues and says that if there is to be a wedding, so be it, but then let it be with Kano. That is what she is asking, there, on her knees, her eyes to the ground. She is glad to be a Djimba, but let it be with the son she loves. She implores Khaya and invokes the spirits of weddings, who will be flattered that love is being offered to them. She speaks and it is to utter the name of Kano. Since it changes almost nothing. No one replies. The silence lasts a long time. She waits some more then slowly, respectfully looks up. Khaya is indeed there. Before her. Surrounded by four or five attendants. They do not move, they are waiting to see what the queen will say. Khaya slowly goes over, never taking her eyes off the young girl. She repeats her sentences one by one. "You will not oppose it?" And Salina knows this means no. "You just want to choose between my two sons?" She knows that what is coming is not only a refusal, but a humiliation as well. Khaya is getting angry, her voice growing louder. "You want to choose?" she asks. "You think you can decide?" Salina is about to repeat Kano's name, just to brandish it against the anger that is coming, but she doesn't have time. Khaya goes on, looks her up and down, and now she is smiling. "Listen to me, Salina," she says, "You will marry my son, and it is my will that it shall be Saro. If you fight it, I will force you. If you bite, or shout, or strike out, I will knock you senseless with my own hands and we will drag you to the altar." And that is not all. She says Salina is nothing. And that she ought to be happy to have been chosen. That Saro will take her and do what he likes with her. She speaks her rage at having been insulted by the girl's request. A long hatred will be born that day, in those moments of cold insults. A long hatred that will last an entire lifetime. Salina gets to her feet, looks Khaya straight in the eye, says nothing more, for there is nothing more to attempt, but she wants the other woman to see, now and for always, her defiance. A long hatred, forever, passing from one to the other.

Before she goes back to Mamambala's hut, where she will stay motionless for three days and three nights, still hoping Khaya will change her mind, praying that Kano will intercede with his mother, before she huddles against Mamambala's side, clenching her teeth, there are the hours she spends in the dry riverbed. She runs out of Khaya's hut, not thinking, just running. She stays there among the branches whitened by the sun and the

dry pebbles at the bottom of the bed of stones. She stag-
gers, turns the words that have just been said over and
over again in her mind. "I will knock you senseless with
my own hands, Salina . . . " Khaya's words in her head.
Everything is laughing, mocking around her. "I'll drag
you with my own two hands if I have to . . . " and the
mother's savage nature goes well beyond the son's. So,
she bends down and picks up a shard of rock. It is as
sharp as a blade. Kill herself? No. She cannot think of
it. She does not want to die. She wants to win against the
Djimbas. What is being born, there, at the bottom of the
dried stream, is her combat. She thinks. If she cuts her
face with this little piece of stone, she will be stripped of
her beauty and Saro will not want her to be his anymore.
All she has to do is slice deep in her cheeks, her brow,
across her nose, her breasts if need be . . . It will hurt so
much she will scream. She will bleed, perhaps faint. The
wounds might get infected and leave her deformed, but
the wedding will go away. Who will want a mutilated
bride? She holds the possibility of escaping her marriage in the palm of her hand, and that freedom has the
shape of a knife. It would be a slap in the face to Khaya
and her son, a slap to all those who are already preparing for the ceremony. She stays like that for a long time,
her fist held tight, imagining the sorrow and everything
that would come of it, but then Kano's face springs to
her mind. She imagines his expression, when he comes
to look at her. And the disgust he will feel . . . Because
if she has to be mutilated, it will be for Kano, too, she
will have to give up everything. So, she lets go of the
sharp stone, which makes a pathetic sound as it hits the
ground, and she retraces her steps, leaving behind her

the pools of blood that will not flow and the gashes that will remain closed.

The day is slow, and the heat is thick as a cloud of dust. The women are busy around her, nervous as birds at the first light of day. They give her yet another necklace. She is already wearing five, but she needs one more. She is wearing earrings so long that they reach her shoulders. Every time she turns her head, the jewelry jangles. She is also wearing gold bracelets of varying thicknesses. She has three on her left forearm and two on her right. One of the women asks her to close her eyes. They put on her makeup. A thousand hands are taking care of her. She says nothing, thinks of nothing, wants everything to stop, but still she has to get dressed. She can see the lengths of fabric, bright, satiny colors, she can tell they are dressing her in them, but she is no longer looking. Perhaps they actually want to make her heavy with all that jewelry? So that she cannot run away. So that it will be impossible to run. They put anklets on her. Whenever she walks, she sounds like a dancer. The women around her seem satisfied. They are smiling, singing, making noise. And then when everything is finished, Khaya comes in, looking like a warlord come to greet his men before the battle. Their gazes do not meet. Khaya is watching her the way one watches an animal that has been prepared for a sacrifice. Everything is in place. "Put on the Tadouk," she says with authority. The women do as they are told. This is the last adornment before the beginning of the ceremony. They take the Tadouk out of a box made of mother-of-pearl. It is a tiara with a long golden chain that fastens to the nostril and bears the sacred signs of virginity. Once she is wearing it, all the girls let out a cry of celebration. "Where is Mamambala?" she wants to ask, but she doesn't have time for her question, for they are already taking her out. The litter is waiting. She climbs into it by herself. Once she is inside, the space is so small that she has to squeeze her knees together. She peers out through the silk curtains, embroidered red and gold. It's hot. Sometimes she can see people. She can hear noise. The litter moves forward with a strangely swaying motion. It is as if she were floating above a crowd, sliding over the shoulders, heads, and backs of all these men. Where are they taking her? She hopes the road will be long, infinitely long. That they will have to carry her to Mount Tadma and far beyond. As long as she is in that chair, she is not married. Never mind if it is hot, if her bracelets are tight . . . Never mind if she is a prisoner of gold and cloth, she is not married. She clenches her teeth to keep from screaming. She knows it will serve no purpose. Then, finally, the litter comes to a halt. The four men who are carrying it lower it to the ground. A hand parts the veil with an abrupt gesture. She recognizes it, it is Khaya's hand. From then on, everything goes very quickly. When she gets out, her legs are aching from having been curled up for so long. Her ankle bracelets jangle with every step she takes. She hardly has time to see the crowd around her. The entire village is there. There are faces she does not know, men who have come from brotherly clans, in the North and the West. Over a hundred men and women crowd around her. They guide her. Her head is spinning. She falters, but someone at her side catches her. Everything has been planned so there can be no signs of weakness. Was it Khaya who ordered for her to be watched so carefully? They lead her to a circle. Saro is there, wearing the Djimba battle dress. On his torso, the sacred signs of the clan have been painted white. Flags have been brought out. There is not a breath of air. Her gaze searches for Kano. It seems to her that his is the only face that would give her strength in this moment, but she cannot find him. Sissoko Djimba begins to speak. He is speaking, but she pays no attention to what he is saying. It all goes very quickly. He has already finished. Now he is pouring some red water on the ground and, all at once, everyone cries out and roars with joy. That's it. She is married. She saw nothing, felt nothing, understood nothing. But it's already done and now Saro is receiving compliments as if he had accomplished a great feat.

It should all have stopped there, with the voluble congratulations of the men calling for prosperity and the clemency of the gods for the newlyweds. But then a man from the clan in the North arrives. He is in a sweat and he interrupts the chanting. He speaks quickly, tensely: an army has been seen near the royal towers, on the first dunes. In one second, the excitement of the wedding is transformed into warlike feverishness. The men reach for their Takouba swords and, without even changing out of their ceremonial costumes, they leave the place. Salina is immediately put back into the litter, as if, since Saro is no longer there, no one must see her. That is when she prays. For the first time. To all the spirits she knows: she prays for the battle to take place, out there, in the sand dunes, beneath the gods' impassive gaze. She prays that the enemies will be numerous and brutal. Stronger. Hungrier. And that they will kill Saro. That they will converge upon him and him alone. That they will sense that he is the

clan's eldest son, and that he is the one who must be slain.
That they will kill him, trample him, transform him into
an unrecognizable body. With all her might, she prays she
will be a widow. In one day, bride and widow. Because
what would happen then is required by tradition: she will
be given to the brother of the deceased, and in a few seconds this accursed wedding day will become the day of
her happiness. She prays. For everything to change, radi-
cally, and be transformed: for misfortune to turn to joy,
and her stolen life to elation. But the spirits are deaf to her
pleas. Or perhaps Khaya prayed more loudly than she did.

A few hours later, the men return. There was no battle.
Only one enemy scout was killed. And it was Saro who
slew him. He still has traces of the victim's blood on his
torso. He is exultant. Everyone describes his exploits,
repeats them, exaggerates them: how he leapt at the man,
brought him to the ground, how his blows were quick and
powerful, how the other man tried to get away and how
Saro caught him, jumped on him a second time, and slit
his throat with his sacred sword. It augured well for the
marriage. All the men were saying it: the gods are with he
who receives an enemy to burn. He smiles, looks at Salina,
who has been taken back out of her litter. Something has
changed in his eyes: now he is staring at her, greedily. She
clenches her fists. May they be cursed, those gods who
have granted none of her wishes and who bend to the will
of the Djimbas. She knows it is time, that nothing more
can prevent what is coming. There will be no war today.
Perhaps tomorrow, but by then it will be too late. Saro
comes closer, seizes her by the arm, and leads her away.
All the men hail his gesture with a sort of savage joy, as if

they dreamt of doing the same thing. She clenches her jaw so that she will not be broken by what lies ahead.

Malaka stops, allows the soft evening air to pass over his face. No one around him moves. Not a sound interrupts the silence. He needs to breathe more deeply. He knows what is coming, he knows what he is going to have to tell. He will have to speak about the body of his mother, who was merely a child, her body which had begun to bleed like a girl, and which could be impregnated like a woman. He will have to speak with sensuality about his mother, about the desire she aroused, the desire she had in herself, and which they all spat on. He is going to do it. He is not afraid. He just has to take his time. The story protects him. When he is immersed in the words, there is no more modesty, no more politeness or consideration. He must simply say what happened. To tone things down would be lying. To attenuate the violence, and not tell of the bodies bleeding, the bodies secreting an enemy flux, not tell of the one's muscles crushing the other, forcing and twisting to take pleasure, would be lying. He has to speak because, for years, those were the details that fed Salina's anger. It is by telling the story of her ravaged body, her body in its raw obscenity, that he will best tell of the affront from which she never recovered, and to which she constantly returned. And so, he begins to speak again, and there is something broken in his voice. "I, Malaka, the son of a woman who was long on her knees, must tell these moments when the bodies of my mother and Saro were pressed together, one inside the other, one weighing on the other and hurting it, crushing it, those moments when a man takes the woman beneath him with voracity, for the simple pleasure not of possessing her—for Saro always knew he would never possess her—but of damaging her. Those moments when, because it will not consent, Salina's body must pay, bear the marks of his blows, submit."

There is neither pleasure nor pain. She tries not to be in her body anymore. She looks at the cloth of her dress, which he has torn and scattered around her. Her necklaces hurt. Saro's torso is weighing upon her and the golden ornaments press into her flesh. She does not cry out, she says nothing. She may as well bleed, it hardly matters . . . Every thrust of his loins kills her a little, in her spirit. She feels him, there, sweating, grunting, tense inside her. She tries to be as uncomfortable as possible, angular and dry. Sometimes he lifts her brusquely, to straighten her pelvis or open her thigh. She puts up no resistance. She knows he would only beat her in return. He moves in and out, puffs, breathes more and more loudly. His sweat drips on her and his smell makes her want to vomit. A little of the enemy scout's blood is now on her breasts, and that seems to excite Saro, since he licks them with his mouth wide open. She recalls the hyenas at the time of her birth. She wishes she could call to them, that they would come into the hut, crowd around the bed and devour Saro . . . But no one comes and he goes on, searching for pleasure from this body that wants nothing to do with him, aroused by the tension in Salina's muscles, her mute reticence. He twists her arm, crushes it. She tries to forget herself. She does not know that not far from there, in the stream, Mamambala is dying. The old woman has just stepped slowly, almost cautiously into the water. This is the day she has chosen to go back to the world of stones, torrents, and the breath of things. Mamambala lets the cloth of her dress float for a while on the surface of the water, then it grows heavy and sinks into the current, and she does the same, going all the way into the water while her daughter clenches her fists until her palms bleed. Saro is feverish, forces her, presses her, takes the breath out of her and she does not know that Mamambala has let herself slip to the bottom of the torrent, her eyes wide open, because for her the world came to an end the moment Salina was taken from her. Saro's breathing takes up all the room. Almost a groan, invading everything with its presence, while Mamambala is asking for her breathing to stop. She is under the water, spirit of the torrent forever. And when at last Saro reaches his climax, and once he has regained his breath and is wiping off the blood that is staining his torso, nothing can ever be as it was. From now on, Salina knows: her name is pain.

There is no ceremony—or barely. According to custom, Mamambala's hut is burned with everything it contains. What people wish to pass on must be given during their lifetime. What they own on the day of their death is burned so that they will take it with them. Salina watches the hut burning, twisting in the flames, then collapsing in a cloud of hot dust and fireflies. She thinks back on all those hours spent in Mamambala's bed, all the rag dolls she had made for her. The men around her are singing and playing the drum. If the deceased had been a man, the women would have sung. They will then wait three times seven days: seven days for the ashes to cool, seven days for the spirits to depart, seven days for the wind to erase the tears, then they will rebuild a small house on the same spot and Mamambala will truly have become a ghost. But Salina cannot wait. She knows that Mamambala is already in the stream. So that is where she goes: she dives slowly into the water to wash, to find again the warmth of her mother, her voice, her softness. She dives to be with her again and speak to her. "I'm not your daughter anymore, Mamambala," she murmurs at the surface of the water, "your voice doesn't surround me anymore, doesn't call to me. I can't find your smell around me anymore. I'm not your daughter anymore and, for my sins, I will soon be a mother myself." And the old woman replies from the depths of the torrent, amid the pebbles polished by the water, "I never was your mother, Salina." Her voice is gentle. "Mothers know, they can sense, whereas all the time I kept you, watched over you, tried to help you grow, I looked at you with a sort of surprise mingled with fear. I'm not your mother, Salina, because I never knew what would come out of you, but I loved you. That's it. I loved you and that's stronger than blood."

The voice falls silent and Salina stays in the water for a long time to avoid going back to the world, seeing those men she hates, going back to the hut that is still burning, to her belly which will grow rounder by the day now. To avoid going back to what will come out of her one day. She knows what it is, what has always been hidden deep inside her, ever since she was a newborn baby: screams, and nothing else.

Malaka falls silent. He takes the time to think about the young woman whose story he is telling. He realizes that he never heard her scream. For as long as he can remember, Salina was silent. She spoke little, she would often look at him for minutes on end while he was eating or was about to fall asleep. Not like a mother who is gazing lovingly at her child, but like a woman who is surprised to realize this child is hers, surprised and grateful. He has always felt this in her: a silent incredulity. Her cries—it is as if she stifled them because they belonged to her life from before. She no longer had the right to scream, no longer the right to rage, she had this son. He always felt he was her reconciliation with the world. Deep down, he realizes he does not know her. She is far away, the other Salina, the one who screamed and was banished. She belongs to another world. Something began with his own birth that propelled that world into a distant country of the desert and old tales. He is talking about a woman he can know nothing about, a woman who would frighten him if he had her there before him. At that moment, emotion overcomes him: he understands that, during her life as a mother, she did everything she could to spare him the screams. She twisted them inside her, silenced them, swallowed them at the back of her throat so as not to convey them to him. She fought so that her son would never know what it meant to have them for his only companions. So, in his mind, he salutes this Salina he is telling, the enraged, violent woman, and thanks her for stepping aside to let him grow up.

VI
THE ANGER SON

The first child is the fruit of rape and does nothing but wail. A little bundle of flesh that depends on her to live, wriggling, crying its lungs out until it is red in the face . . . They place it next to her, thinking she will give it her warmth, but she looks at it without moving. The infant puts all his life force into his crying. She seems not to hear him. Is it possible that she is remembering her own crying on the roads of her exile, when the horseman was carrying her? Is it possible that she feels at home, surrounded by his crying? Saro named him Mumuyé and the entire clan joyfully celebrated his birth. The lineage is assured. The bloodline will be perpetuated. She did not oppose anything, nor did she consent. When they placed the infant in her arms, she did not even look at him. She waited a bit, then placed him in a blanket at her side. When he needs to suckle, she takes him, unfastens her garment, places him at her breast, and looks away. She does not want to see him, does not want to grow tender, does not want to register any of this childhood. He is the son of the beating she has taken inside, the son of violence, and that is all. He is the hated blood of Saro and the image of her own submission. She feeds him because she knows that if she doesn't, they will beat her, but she doesn't care if he cries. She thinks of Kano, whom she sees only very rarely, when the entire clan comes together for a meal or a wake and then she looks at him, not saying a word, gazing at his beauty, her eyes full of desire, smiling sometimes so he will know that, in spite of everything, she is his and that nothing else exists in her. But often he lowers his eyes. Then she is filled with rage and her face hardens. Why didn't he say something? Why didn't he oppose his brother or mother? He heard the sound of thrusting on the wedding night—everyone heard—and he did nothing. Perhaps he wept or buried his head in the cushions, but that is even worse . . . In fact, little Mumuyé is also the son of Kano's cowardice, and that is yet another reason to let the infant cry. Mumuyé's cries go with her everywhere, all the time. And Saro strolls about, beside himself, scowling, furious at the child's crying, furious at this affront. He orders Salina to make the infant stop. "Give him what he wants. Your milk. Your arms. Give him your time, your body," he says, his face red with anger. "If this son cries, imagine that it is me crying. If he is hungry, it is I who is hungry. You must dread what I will do if I am not satisfied. Will you do it grudgingly? You want to be slow, make him wait? So be it. That is fine with me. Then he will feel in his little self that you don't want him, that you are no sort of mother, but something is forcing you, something greater than you are, stronger, and you have submitted to it, something that protects him and watches over him despite your neglect, and he will understand that this force is his father." She smiles on hearing these words, takes the child slowly in her arms and answers with a defiant pout. "I have picked him up, look. I am feeding him, yes. But he will have no part of me. Nothing of what a mother gives. I will never say the name you have given him. I will never speak to him. Let him feel that I am bending to your will, that is fine with me. That way he will understand that if he has a mother it is out of obedience, and that will tear him apart forever."

Saro goes out, brimming with rage, and for a few seconds the child's crying stops.

Malaka breaks off as if he wanted little Mumuyé's crying to echo into the night. Darzagar looks at him with a new expression. He is captivated by the story, Malaka can tell. And so, the young man continues. "I, Malaka, son of the woman who hated her child, cannot tell the long chain of slowly passing days, and yet I must. I cannot find a word for every moment of everyday life that is a threat, a humiliation, an act of violence, and yet I must, to describe the torture caused by this sensation of slow death, locked up in a life that has been forced upon you. To describe the violence of a word, a blow. Saro's presence is nothing but brutality. I must describe everything: the wearing down, the anger, and the sadness of every day. I must, otherwise it will be impossible to understand how hatred accumulates. The youth that is torn from her, her ravaged body. The face that is constantly humiliated. I must find the words for this: the feeling that, from now on, life will be nothing but resignation, and that it will be long, infinitely long, until the grave."

War has returned. It has been hovering like a fly, coming and going, threatening. The kingdom of the South has a renewed appetite and wants to subjugate the towns in the desert. Perhaps they aim to get their hands on the great caravanserais, and control the spice trade? Perhaps King Sal'Elmaya has merely taken a dislike to the Djimbas and has sworn to reduce them to ashes? Years go by, and skirmishes are increasingly frequent. And then, on the day of Mumuyé's thirteenth birthday, they prepare for the first great battle. Sal'Elmaya is marching on the Djimba lands. Mumuyé is almost old enough to fight. Saro wants him to—so that his son will be an accomplished man as soon as possible—but Khaya is against it. She says curtly to her eldest son that he must go alone onto the battlefield. He does not insist, he is too busy getting ready. His Takouba sword never leaves his hand, and every morning he draws the insignia of death on his face, red and white colors to frighten the enemy before he kills them. War has returned and has taken possession of everything. Until the day the battle is announced. The enemy is very near. A nervous agitation spreads from one hut to the next. Old Sissoko gathers everyone together. He announces that the day for the attack has come and that, this time, it is his sons Kano and Saro who will lead the men into battle. Everything is ready and the men are already running—as if there were nothing more beautiful than imminent death.

She is in the middle of the village, tense, immobile. All the warriors have left the camp. They left many long minutes ago and surely by now have reached the place where they will fight. She tries to imagine the first clashes between Sal'Elmaya's warriors and the Djimbas. At every instant, she wonders whether Saro is in the tangle of bodies, whether—at this very moment, as she is drawing in breath—he is striking or has been struck . . . It is a day of blood; she can feel it. It is something she has always been able to feel, her senses aroused, a drumming in her veins that makes her want to bite, to dance, to cry out. It is a day of blood, and perhaps today Saro will die. She tries to imagine the enemy warriors surrounding him, the blows he will stave off, in the beginning, and then with encroaching fatigue, his first wounds: he lowers his guard, it becomes harder and harder to breathe, his gestures are less precise, his assaults weaker. She tries to imagine it: an enemy she will never know, but to whom she gives her blessing, goes up to Saro and with a brutal gesture cuts off his head or plunges a sword into his belly, right up to the hilt. She wants it to be true. It is a day of blood, she can feel it, so she is anxious, wonders whether it might not be Kano who is dying. The very thought torments her, the image of Kano on his knees in the dust . . . She cannot stand it anymore, she has to see, she has to know, so she flouts the ancestral rule that says women are to wait for the warriors in the village, and she runs to the battlefield.

She runs, and distance no longer matters, heat no longer matters. If today is to be the day of her liberation, she is prepared to run to the farthest corners of the desert. Before long, the hill of stones is before her. She knows the battlefield is on the other side, she can tell from the smell. Birds have already begun to circle. She climbs as best she can, using her hands, clutching at stones, she climbs and then, once she has reached the crest, she sees the great dying-place of war: an ugly succession of broken, moaning bodies. The same men who a few hours ago left with proud smiles, the same men who promised strife to their enemies are there, disfigured, already cold, astonished to be the ones who are lying on the ground and not the victors. The battle is already over. It is impossible to tell who has won and who has lost. The warriors have left the battlefield. Only the dying remain. She climbs over bodies. "Let him be here," she says to herself, repeatedly, in a low voice. She observes the faces, sometimes stops to turn over a corpse, she is afraid of nothing anymore, "Let him be here," and suddenly she freezes. A dozen yards from her, on his back, his head toward the slope, she recognizes him right away: it is Saro's body. At first, she doesn't dare move, she cannot believe her eyes, then she goes closer, timidly, dreading she might find she is mistaken, but the closer she gets the more she recognizes the details of his armor, his leggings, until now she sees his face. His mouth open, groaning, his eyes staring wide at the circling birds, a big gaping wound in his belly, it is Saro. Today is a day of blood. She goes even closer, right up to him, so that he can see her. She does not lean over him, she remains upright. Her shadow makes him blink. He turns his head slightly. "Can you see me, Saro?" she asks eagerly. "Look. I'm not moving." She stands very straight. "I'm smiling. All I have to do is do nothing for you to die. Look, Saro, I am leaving you to what you have always liked best: war, blood, and violence. Can you see me? Yes, I know you can see me, you made a face. I will outlive you, Saro, I am going to get away from your brutality. My life will no longer be governed by your will. You are dying, Saro, and the last face you will see will be mine, but you can hardly recognize it because it has been set free from what you were." And Saro doesn't move, doesn't speak, probably no longer has the strength to say even a single word, or perhaps he didn't understand what she was saying, just heard the tone of her voice, her teeth clenched, the victory of her suppressed rage, and so he finally does what the birds have been waiting for, what Salina and the entire world have been waiting for: he stiffens and dies. She stands there motionless for a while, attentive, as if she wanted to make sure he would not come back. She waits, fills herself with this new silence, then all of a sudden, she turns away and starts running—running as she has not done since she was a child—running as fast as her legs will carry her. She leaves the battlefield and Saro's body, she leaves the birds, which are circling closer to earth now because they are singling out the bodies they have decided to target. She goes straight to the village and nothing frightens her anymore. Saro is dead and the ancestral rules will give her the life she has been hoping for.

Once she reaches the village, she stands outside the great hut of the Djimbas and begins to intone the lament of bereavement. "Aya, aya, my husband is dead . . . Aya, aya, his vigor was lost on the battlefield . . . " She sings ardently, and already everyone is coming out into the street. The news spreads: Saro is dead . . . ? The women ask the question in a low voice to the warriors who were there. Some confirm they did indeed see him fall, "Aya, aya, may you weep: the warriors fallen today will not see the new day break," the crowd swells around her. Saro is dead and their faces are pale. She goes on. She is not afraid of anything anymore, she sings, "Aya, aya, add the name of my husband to the list of the Glorious, for he is no more," and, finally, old Khaya appears. She is in mourning dress. She asks no questions, does not doubt any of Salina's words. Perhaps she has already heard the news, or perhaps she felt the death in her gut the moment Saro was struck? She stands straight before Salina. The men come up, too, the warriors back from battle, the wounded. Kano is there next to his father. Salina was waiting for this: for the entire village to be there. It is time to erase the suffering, to set aside the misfortune that has constantly surrounded her life, "Aya, aya," she does not take the time to ask someone to bring her husband's body to her, she does not want to pretend to weep over him. She will not fall to her knees in the dust in lamentation, shaking her head and plunging her hands in the wound to cover her face with the blood of the man who has died, or to feel his warmth one last time, she will not do any of the things that widows do, and Khaya knows it. Salina is there before her and it is not to weep, it is to deliver the final blow, to slap her in the face before everyone, to avenge the affront of the marriage, the affront of Mumuyé's birth, and of every wound she ever received, and so she goes on chanting, "Aya, aya," she knows she is protected by the ancestral rules of the village, which even Khaya Djimba must abide by, "through the death of my husband, I am left without a man, and the son who was born to me by Saro is left without a father. The gods of our village do not want this." She turns to Khaya, looks her straight in the eye. "Khaya, owing to the death of Saro, I ask for your second son to be my husband. May I become the wife of Kano, since I must remain a Djimba." And the old woman does not move, receives Salina's words like a slap, but knows she cannot oppose them. Kano opens his mouth wide, does not know whether to weep for his brother or encourage Salina. The entire village is listening, hanging on her every word. "Aya, aya, Khaya, by the ancestral rules, you cannot refuse: I must be Kano's wife." Salina is facing the clan, her head held high, her gaze riveted on this woman who has been nothing but hatred. Life will change, at last. What was torn from her will be returned. The endless games with Kano, the gentleness of a caressing hand, the children to be born, who will have names, who will be a path toward wonder. If Kano asks her to, she will even try to love Mumuyé, she will put all her heart into it and try even harder. She cannot take her eyes off the old woman. She has hoped so often for this victory. She does not see that the faces around her have turned toward the road outside the village. She does not hear the murmur running through the crowd. She thinks everything will be all right. And it is only when a voice rings out that she turns and sees a strange man dressed in rags who has bowed down respectfully before Sissoko to greet him and who is smiling now, awkwardly.

"Sissoko Djimba, son of Moussouké Djimba, descendant of the lineage of panther killers, listen to me. It is I, Oulgo the madman, who is speaking to you," he says, and Salina senses that misfortune has come again. "I am a hermit and I live at the edge of the village, everyone will tell you that. I speak to the pebbles. There are nights when I shout out loud to make the stars dance." Oulgo speaks and everyone listens. They know him. Some give him alms, or the remains of their meals on days of plenty. The women sometimes leave clothes for him in the hills and he grabs them, the way a wild beast pounces on its prey, but most of the time he goes around half-naked, half-hairy, feeding on insects and speaking to his own body as if it were a crowd. That is what he does now, while everyone surrounds him, waiting to see what he has come to say, and he exhorts his lips to continue. "Speak, mouth . . . speak, since you know the words," he says, "Ask your eyes what they have seen and tell us . . . " And so, he continues. "Sissoko, you know me, I keep away from you because I don't smell the same as men. Your lives are too noisy for me. I am a scavenger in the desert, a licker of stones. The ants feed me, and I ask for nothing. But when men make war and kill each other, I have a feast. So many bodies, so many belongings, satchels, supplies. I lick whatever is flowing and gather up the rest. The dead are not stingy. I am like the birds as they glide patiently above your massacres. And today again, a great battlefield, a feast of bodies. I walk. From one to the other. I wait for it all to finish. I grow rich on what the dead have left. I take, I carry, I check what it is in the bags. But I always wait for the dying to be dead, otherwise it is theft. May both my hands be cut off if ever I took anything from the living."

The men and women of the village are beginning to wonder what the hermit is trying to say. Salina clenches her fists. Something is approaching, she can tell, something threatening. And the smile spreading across Khaya's face makes her even more worried.

"I was there where the killing was today. After the attack came the time for dying. I went from one body to the next. I saw your son, Saro, on the ground. I was very near to him, but I didn't take anything. He was still alive, I swear, and I'm not a thief—you already said so, lips—I wait for the dead to give of their own free will. Saro was breathing, blinking, I could see. I went away. And then, I saw her, too," and he pointed at Salina, "and she—show where she is, finger!—she went over to him, I swear, when he was still alive. She spoke to him, I don't know what words she used because I was too far away, but I saw her: she didn't bend down, she didn't help him, nothing. She was there, with her husband before her eyes, dying, and it might have still been possible to drag him, to save him, still, surely, but she stood there straight, and let his blood flow without trying to dress his wound, I tell you, she's the one, I swear, the wife who did nothing. And that is what I, Oulgo, came to say, before I go back to my stones."

Everyone turns all at once toward Salina. She does not flinch. She knows that everything is about to vanish: her hopes of a gentle life, Kano's hands, the children who would be born of a joyful bed. Everything is vanishing and still she has to drink the glass down to the dregs, still she has to see Khaya's face light up with a savage glow and hear her words of a lioness when she explodes. "You, cursed woman! You thought you could come here and get my second son? You thought you could humiliate me, spit on my name, and dance on Saro's still warm body?" And still she has to see Sissoko's gesture, as he raises his arm so that all will be silent, and speaks, his voice icy with outrage: "I, Sissoko Djimba, offended father, I will say it: I should kill you with my own hands, Salina, to avenge Saro. I ought to make sure that no stone will ever cover your corpse since you have brought nothing but desolation to this village. But I cannot. Wild gods whom we know nothing about are protecting you. Gods who may be waiting for nothing more than an act of blood on our part to swoop down on our village and kill us all. You come from so far away that no one knows. Only tears are a certainty with you, Salina. I will not kill you, but I will banish you. Let the desert do with you what it wants. You will have solitude and wandering. We will keep Mumuyé and raise him in the memory of his father. We will keep Mumuyé who has never been your son."

Still she has to hear these words and see Kano's face as he says nothing, lowers his eyes, does not try to go against fate, to convince the clan that Salina did not kill Saro, that it was war that killed him. Still she has to endure the disgust dawning in everyone's eyes. Still she must submit again to the women's spitting, once Sissoko pronounces the banishment, and the warriors who go up to her, roughly, implying to her that they will escort her to her hut and give her time to take a few belongings, then they will force her to leave, and they will follow her until she has left the lands of the Djimba behind. Still she has to know all this, for her to feel that her entire life has just been stolen from her.

Only then, once she is alone, once she is beyond the land that she knows, when the warriors have turned their backs on her and gone away again, marching heavily toward the village, only then can she scream. But she does not open her mouth to scream. She feels as if her anger cannot get past her jaws. It is greater, more immoderate. She walks, for days and nights, letting the scream well up inside her. She no longer eats, or eats only grasses stolen from the sun. She only drinks by lifting stones that hide tiny torrents. She licks the pebbles to retrieve the infinitesimal leavings of dew, and she begins to swell, then grows bigger and bigger. Something is coming to life in these days of solitude. It comes and goes, and her belly continues to grow. It does not take nine months for her to give birth to what she is carrying, but nine days. At the end of the ninth day of exile, she lies back against a sand dune, and what was growing inside her can come out at last. She cries out, like a woman giving birth, dripping with sweat, her legs spread. She pushes with all her strength and gives birth to her anger child. Nine days of pregnancy for Koura Kumba to be born. He does not come out the way Mumuyé came out, like a little puppy, red with the effort of living, he comes out like a man, already. Koura Kumba, fully formed, whom she expels on that dune on the ninth night of her second exile. She has a son, now, all to herself, a son who is taller and stronger than any of the warriors in the village. She welcomes him, cherishes him, embraces him. She has a son who will be the secret weapon of her revenge.

VII
THE COMBAT OF THE BROTHERS

Malaka falls silent. He has been speaking for several hours and the first light of day is appearing on the horizon. There are many boats around them now. Not all are tied together like the first two. Some are following, others escort them alongside. He looks at this little flotilla of fishermen and traders with their colorful sails, and he seems unsure of what he should do. Old Darzagar sees his hesitation and says:

"The story of the deceased must only be told at night. Spirits disappear during the day to let the city live. You can rest. Regain your strength, if you want."

He had not noticed, but there is renewed bustle and activity on board the boats. All around, the women are busy, passing bowls from hand to hand. The boats have regrouped and almost all of them are touching one another. Bags are passed over the side and exchanged. He gets the impression that the entire city is there on the water, that the entire city has come to hear his story, taking a pause in its city life. The fisherman's wife shows him three bowls of different colors. In one, there is a cold poultry soup. In the next, some rice, and in the third, a fruit he does not recognize, but which the woman has already peeled. He thanks her and begins to eat.

Sleep comes quickly to Malaka. A thick linen canvas

has been rigged between the mast and the stern of the boat to provide some shade, and he becomes drowsy. He tries for a while to stay awake to gaze at the shore of the islands as they come nearer, but he fails. And in those moments when sleep begins to dull him, he hears the bustle all around: those who have not heard Salina's story, or those who were too far away to catch the words he was saying, have come closer now, and ask others to repeat what was told during the night. The fishermen repeat everything, with earnest voices, trying to reconstruct the slightest details; sometimes they are corrected by others, more vigilant, who seek to clarify an episode. And in this way, he falls asleep, surrounded by a hundred murmuring voices repeating and spreading the story of the woman he is taking to the cemetery.

When he wakes a few hours later, the boat is being rocked by the rolling of the waves. The sun has disappeared, and the daylight is fading before his eyes. The entire flotilla has come to a halt and is visibly waiting for him to go on with his story. And so, he begins to speak again, and this is the second night of words:

"I, Malaka, son of a mother who brought her child alone into the world, I am continuing the story of Salina, whom I left in the sand, for it is in the sand, always, that she lived. Koura Kumba was born and he was eager to fight. She brought him into the world for that purpose alone. I am evoking this brother I never knew, but whom she told me about so many times, her eyes always weeping with pride and sadness. I say 'brother' without knowing whether Koura Kumba really was my brother. Because we did not have the same mother. The woman who gave birth to him was fixed on her desire to sting. She wanted to make the dunes bleed. He was born for that. So that the vengeance might begin and the Djimbas would be punished."

Koura Kumba is bigger than most men. Bare-chested, with a dark gaze and his face wrapped in long cloths to protect him from the sandstorms, he seems to have been born to defy the sun. Salina oiled his body herself and fashioned a Takouba sword for him from desert stones. She filed this weapon for hours, until her fingers bled, so that it would be as sharp as possible. When everything is ready, he kisses her hands and leaves the dune where he was born. Now the long trek through the desert begins, a trek made of nothing but defiance, assault, and blood. He raids the traders' caravans, bars their way, and kills or burns anything bearing the Djimba insignia. Salina taught him how to recognize them. Everything along the road is put to fire and sword. Everywhere he goes he says his name, Koura Kumba, the son of Salina and of her anger, so that it might be repeated and all will know that a strange creature has come to provoke Sissoko and his family. What he does not know is that the war between the Djimbas and Sal'Elmaya has intensified. Battles are raging for the control of the trading posts. In the beginning, he is taken for a warrior from the South, a mercenary more terrifying than all the others. He does not want to be mistaken for one of Sal'Elmaya's men, and that is why he says his name, repeats it endlessly. "Koura Kumba," he says, and this name eventually reaches Sissoko's ears, and he turns pale. The Djimba chief sends three of his best warriors to look for the man who, it is

said, was born from the dunes. They return shortly there-
after, in a cart drawn by a donkey. All three have been
slain, their bodies riddled with stab wounds. Koura
Kumba left them no chance, and he mutilated their
remains so that everyone would tremble at the sight of
what he can do. Sissoko can sense that there is something
here that cannot be explained, but his mind is busy with
Sal'Elmaya's attacks. That seems more urgent to him, but
he is wrong. He does not prepare for their combat, and
yet the combat arrives. It is near the stream that the two
men meet. Face-to-face, at last. Sissoko has grown old. He
is no longer the warrior he once was. Koura Kumba
slowly looks him over, smiles, and challenges him. He tells
him his name. He tells him who gave him birth. He tells
him how he is going to strike him. "Death has come for
you, Sissoko." He tells him that death will not be the end
of his suffering, that Salina's vengeance requires more.
That he will have no rest. "Torment has come for you,
Sissoko," since Salina has been condemned to exile. He
tells him that after Sissoko's life, he will take the lives of
all the warriors in his clan, right down to Mumuyé, so that
the entire lineage will weep blood. "Tears have come for
you, Sissoko." He tells him all this with a sovereign voice
then, once he has said everything, before the old man has
time to react, he moves toward him and with a wide
sweep of his arm and the desert-sharpened sword, he cuts
off his head. There was nothing Sissoko could do. The
blow was too quick, the hand too steady, and his life
escapes, gushes out from his severed head. But that is not
enough. Salina has told him: vengeance requires more.
And so, Koura Kumba kneels by the still-warm body and,
with a sharp gesture, slices open the old man's corpse, the

way one guts a fish, and tears out his spinal column, with the dull sounds of flesh profaned. Then he takes it with him as if he were dragging a long bloody snake behind him. Later, Khaya will weep. Not over Sissoko's death— for he was killed as a warrior—but over his open body, left to the beasts. Khaya will weep over the dismembered vengeance that has left Sissoko forever incomplete. There is no rest for a corpse that is not whole. There is no rest in long eternity for those who have been amputated.

When Koura Kumba comes back to the encampment, Salina sees to the offering he has brought her. She prepares a fire and places the spinal column on it so it will be purged of its flesh. Then she rolls it in the sand and delicately detaches each vertebra. Twenty-four vertebrae, twenty-four little bones which she places in a leather bag. Her victory fits in the palm of her hand and sounds like pebbles clicking together. Once the ceremony is over, she looks eagerly at the vertebrae and says to her son:

"Look, my son, this is what, from now on, they will be searching for everywhere. They will be ready to cover every plot of land, to dig in the sand of the dunes to find their father's bones. I will hide them one by one in the four corners of the desert, in places only I know of. I will bury them in the sand, and the dunes themselves will end up forgetting them. Look, my son: so that the last vertebra will be in the most inaccessible place on earth, I am giving it to you. You will wear it around your neck, and no one, ever, will be able to take it because no one, ever, will be able to defeat you. Even if the Djimbas manage to find all the others, they will always be missing this one, and old Sissoko will go about with his head bowed for all eternity, remembering Salina's sting."

At Sissoko's funeral, no one sings. None of the sacred prayers are said, Khaya has forbidden it. She knows that her husband will not rest in peace. It took two days for the women to stitch the remains together, placing fragrant herbs in the wounds. "Bury him seated on his golden stool," she ordered. And the men did as she told them. They dug deep into the earth. Then with careful gestures, they seated their chief. "And so, he will wait," explains Khaya. "Until I bring back what was stolen from him." And while the wind gently rises, sweeping away the location of the tomb, she tells everyone that she is leaving, she will no longer be queen, a new world is beginning, and the power has been handed down now to Kano. It has fallen to him to attend to the fate of the Djimbas, to him to wage war against Sal'Elmaya's men. And Kano says nothing, accepting his tasks in silence, and that very evening, in his hut, he gives his instructions to conduct the battle. He has long thought that the Djimba clan cannot face the kingdom of the South alone, and that they must send envoys to all the friendly trading posts, so that all the caravanserais will unite in the fight against the advance of the armies of the South. He knows that, from now on, this is what he must apply himself to, that he will live only for this war. He will be judged in the light of his victories or his failures. As for Mumuyé, he did not get up to go and join the warriors in his uncle's hut. He has another destiny in store. There is a name calling to him in the distance, a name that makes him wince. He reaches for his Takouba sword and says farewell to the village.

There is a name murmured to him, ceaselessly, from his grandfather's tomb, where the old man is seated, head bowed, and that name is Koura Kumba.

Now war has come. Sal'Elmaya's army is advancing. The desert roads are in flames. The clans are clashing, relentlessly. Sal'Elmaya has taken several caravanserais and is trying to cut off the central road that allows the Djimbas to communicate with their allies. Kano knows that he will only win if he bedevils his enemies. He descends with his warriors upon Sal'Elmaya's men during the night, killing their animals, destroying their water supplies, then disappearing. They know the desert. What to their invaders is a furnace is, to them, a fallback position. All the roads are fought over. Bodies lie in the middle of nowhere, the sign of southern attacks and ambushes. War is there, everywhere. Only Mumuyé walks on without regard for the armed groups he passes. He is obsessed by one thing only: finding his half-brother, and never mind if the world is burning around him. Koura Kumba eventually learns that his brother is on his trail. The scorpions tell him so. The shrubbery, the water running beneath the earth tell him so. "Mumuyé is looking for you and is getting closer . . . " And so, he chooses the highest hill, Mount Sékélé, he lights a fire at its summit that will be visible from as far away as possible, and he waits for his enemy to come to him.

The day arrives when the two brothers are face-to-face, taut with the same hatred. Each one wants his share of blood. What Koura Kumba sees in Mumuyé is Saro's arrogant face, so often described to him by Salina. He senses the confidence of a man who was born to a lineage of heirs. He senses Khaya's pride, the scorn of an entire clan, and this inflames him. What Mumuyé sees in Koura Kumba is the unnatural, barbarian child, not born of any father, but from the womb of an exiled woman. It is the ignominy of the man who defiled the body of old Sissoko. And as if that were not enough, Koura Kumba is taunting him, showing him the pendant he wears around his neck, explaining that that is where he keeps his grandfather's last vertebra. Mumuyé could tear him to pieces with his bare hands, but he knows that is not the way the combat must be fought. And so, he sits by the fire, pours his libation on the earth, and takes out his Takouba sword. Koura Kumba does the same. They are face-to-face, their torsos strapped with leather, war paint all over their bodies. And when, finally, they grapple with each other, Mount Sékélé vibrates with a dull thud, as if two stones had just collided.

Every blow is dodged. Every attack is warded off. How long can a fight last? Hours go by and neither one has managed to hurt the other. Their strength is such that every step raises a cloud of dust, every assault causes the ground to tremble. They do not weaken. Neither one loses his composure. They fight with equal force, equal intelligence, equal agility. How long can a fight last? Their blows do not tire, and the hours are worn away, filling with so much hatred.

Finally, it is the sun that yields. It withdraws like an exhausted man. Koura Kumba and Mumuyé do not need to speak. Each one of them knows it is time to interrupt the combat. Each one steps back with a similar motion so that neither one can accuse the other of cowardice, and they sit thirty steps away from each other. There will be no surprise slitting of the throat, no treachery, no sudden attack. Once they have laid down their Takouba swords, everything is interrupted. And then each one drinks, regains his strength, astonished he is not yet the victor, surprised that, on this first night of combat, he is admiring the other's valor, his qualities as a warrior.

How long can a fight last? Every day they get up again, pour their libation, and charge at each other. Every day, they fight with all their strength. Neither one has ever seen as much strength as in his enemy's arm. They are brothers, there can be no doubt about that. They can see it. They master combat with the same artfulness. Sometimes, one of them makes the other fall and roll in the dust—but he gets up. Sometimes, a sword nicks the other's flesh, but it is never more than a scratch. They do not hold each other at a distance, in no way are they sparing of their might. They resort to every ruse, but the only thing that comes of the passing hours is respect for one another, and the thought, perhaps, that when two brothers fight, they can only die together from one and the same blow.

The days go by and they continue striking, looking for the weak spot, trying to deceive the adversary with a dodge, a withholding movement, or a complicated series of moves. The days go by, the second, the third, the fourth. The dust never settles. The birds no longer fly over Mount Sékélé, they think the cloud of dust is a sandstorm. The days go by, the sixth, the seventh, the same alternation of effort, sweat, and silence at nightfall.

Nothing else exists, only combat. The hyenas, lured by the promise of a body soon to be undone, eventually come closer. They sit in a semicircle, waiting for the moment when one of the two men will fall to the ground; or perhaps they're simply curious to see who will triumph. But the days go by and even the hyenas grow weary and, sensing that neither of the two men will destroy the other, they finally go away.

On the ninth day of combat, Mount Sékélé vanishes. The two brothers have hammered the ground so hard that the mountain has collapsed. It has entered the earth, worn down by all those stamping feet, all those attacks, dodges, jumps. They are still fighting, their bodies are thinner, their faces tense. Every day they resume the fight and every day they find a brother there to ward off their attacks. On the ninth day, the combat comes to an end. Because in the place of men, it is the wind that decides. It is Koura Kumba's hundredth, thousandth assault, neither stronger nor more infallible than the previous ones, but just when Mumuyé is about to parry, the wind blows up the sand and blurs his vision. The son of Saro is ill prepared to parry, has left too much room between his sword and his thighs, and Koura Kumba's blade slides effortlessly into his flesh and opens his belly. Mumuyé is surprised and does not immediately feel the pain—just a huge weakness, as if everything were escaping from him. And Koura Kumba, understanding that were it not for the wind that has just turned, his blow would have been parried, understanding that his victory is the fruit of nothing but a strange accident, Koura Kumba, as if this were shameful to him, is left without a voice, without joy, and when Mumuyé puts one knee to the ground, instead of cutting his head off as he had sworn he would do, all through the nine days of combat gone by, he crouches by his side and supports him. The two brothers embrace and speak for the first time. Koura Kumba tells Mumuyé not to die, that he has never seen a combat like theirs. That if he dies, it is because the wind decided to kill him. Otherwise, where did the shame that has gripped Koura Kumba come from, this impression of being victorious without having defeated him? And Mumuyé replies that he is dying, but that he knows it is the wind that has killed him. And that he is filled with rage not for losing to Koura—because he has seen his bravery—but for being removed from the fight. He replies, and it is to say that Koura is a brother, he felt it with every blow he delivered, with every attack thwarted, he says it, that word, utters it, "brother," he says, too, that it is with that word on his lips that he will die. And Koura receives it, that word, he has felt it too, no sooner had they begun to clash. From the same blood, the same valor, indefatigable and upright, "brothers," and it is that word that brings him to his knees to hold with love the body he has killed.

He buries his brother of the last day. He lays out his body carefully, places Mumuyé's Takouba sword on his torso, and sets about covering him. For nine days, the same length of time their combat lasted, he adds sand and rocks, to make his brother a tomb. He spares no effort, sweating as the sun appears. Koura Kumba alone with the stones. He is there, breathless, sweating, moving blocks that no one else could have moved. And at the end of the ninth day, Mount Sékélé reappears, but it is no longer a mountain, it is a mausoleum, the offering from Koura Kumba to Mumuyé Djimba.

When Salina sees her son returning in the evening light, she immediately recognizes him, his magnificent, enormous mass. She sees he is not limping, does not seem to have been touched by any wound. And so, she knows he has won. If he is coming back to her, it means the men of the Djimba clan have paid. But she feels no joy. The closer he comes, the more she can tell this is not a day for celebration. Koura Kumba goes up to her, drinks the water she holds out to him, lets her remove the leather straps he has not taken off for days, and when night has fallen and the air is cool around them, he begins to speak. He tells of the combat, the first blows given. He tells of the powerful hatred that dominated everything. He says that every blow would have sufficed to split open a wall. He tells her how surprised he was to see the way Mumuyé held his own, did not give in, parried every blow and even put him in difficulty. He speaks, and says how sharp Mumuyé was, how his eyes shone. Salina listens and does not respond. She knows what he is going to say. That gradually, bit by bit, as the days went by, they began to feel like brothers. In the beginning, the feeling was troubling. Each one tried to bury it deep inside, to stifle it in order to concentrate fully on his hatred, thinking that the only way to victory was through hatred. "Brother," he says again, looking surprised, like a child, and Salina clenches her jaw because what he is saying is that she had a son, Mumuyé. She would like to ask him to be quiet, to let the sky simply cover them in its silence, but she cannot. She knows that Koura Kumba must say his piece. He tells her about the nine days he spent building the Mount Sékélé mausoleum. He explains to his mother that his body needed to be constantly making an effort, otherwise he would have torn his eyes out from pain. He had never felt this: such a great absence. And when at last he comes to the end of his story, in a clear, serene voice he tells Salina what she has been dreading to hear: that with the death of Mumuyé, everything is finished. That word, "brother," which he accepted, that word has now taken him with it, has shaken him, doomed him to solitude, overwhelmed him, and it is indeed, "We shall die from the same wound," he says, and he adds that it would have been more just had he died on the same day, letting their blood mingle, but now he understands that the delay was not about his victory, but about his duty: it enabled him to offer his brother a tomb. Koura Kumba falls silent. Slowly, he goes up to his mother, nestles against her, his big warrior's body folded into a mother's arms. They are no longer facing each other, but looking up at the stars together. Only Koura Kumba's voice unites them. He speaks and she knows that everything is finished, that she can only accept what he asks of her, he feels it and then he makes his request. She holds her child's body ever tighter in her arms. "I am asking you to take me back, Salina," says Koura Kumba, the anger child, and Salina bites her lips. "May this night be the last. You alone can put an end to my life. No warrior, ever, will be able to kill me, and you know it. I am asking you to take me back." And she knows that there is no point in refusing, and so she does it, she squeezes harder and harder. He feels her embrace, he knows that she is strong, she will go through with it, to the end, he smiles and says a few more words, to help her, to offer her a little bit more of his voice, "I was only the vengeance child, Salina, everything has been done." She would like to weep, but she does not, she listens to his voice giving her courage. "You will bury me beneath that dune and for all eternity I will feel the gentle rolling of the sand. The dunes move forward, you know, like slow ships, and they will take me with them . . . " He says, "Squeeze, mother," and she does, "squeeze to relieve my sadness," and she squeezes forcefully, as tense as an old tree trunk. He has trouble breathing, but does not struggle. She grips him with all her might, with her arms, her legs, she squeezes since that is what he has asked. To the end . . . She takes him back, all of him, her anger son, she squeezes him to feel his last breath, she squeezes him until suddenly his body goes stiff, then immediately relaxes: something has evaporated, she can tell, it's over, all that is left is the immensity of the sky and her own cry, and she lets it out at last.

VIII
THE LAST VERTEBRA

Malaka falls silent. He is exhausted. Something has distressed him in what he has just told them. He always knew of Koura Kumba's existence, and of the circumstances of his death—it was Salina herself who had told him the story—but having to tell it himself has left him dazed. He could feel the tension in Salina's legs, how tight they held on, squeezing even though it filled her with horror, squeezing when all she wanted was to stop, squeezing like a warrior and weeping like a mother. Darzagar looks at him calmly. Slowly, he hands him a bowl of water.

"You don't have to continue the story right away . . . We have all night."

To let his mind rest, Malaka asks the old ferryman how many bodies he has already accompanied to the cemetery.

"You are the first," answers the old man.

Malaka is surprised. He thought his ferryman did it all the time. Darzagar explains that each boatman only ever takes one body. It has always been like that. They settle on the great square and wait. There are times when the body appears after a few hours, sometimes only months, or years. No one can know. But each boatman does it only once. They are men without family, who have reached the age beyond life. When they decide to become ferrymen, they know that this is all they will do: wait for those who come from afar.

"How long did you wait?" Malaka asks.

"Two years," replies Darzagar. And nothing shows on his face, and so Malaka cannot tell whether he is sorry Malaka has taken so long or, on the contrary, whether he would have preferred to have more time.

"Why don't you transport your own dead to the cemetery?" the young man asks.

Darzagar looks astonished by this question.

"Our dead return to the river. That's the way it has always been. They float, decompose, feed the eternal cycle of the waters. The cemetery was built only for strangers. As long as the city has been the city, it has been eager for stories."

And now Malaka feels that he is ready to go on. The city is eager. The ears, eyes, and mouths around him are there to listen, and he must give them the story he has brought from so far away.

Patiently, with a widow's slowness, Khaya searched. She dug in every corner of the desert. Nothing could defeat her tenacity. She looked for traces, observed broken branches, lifted stones, explored wells, sniffing like a dog for the smell of her man, and eventually she found what she was looking for. Patiently, she found twenty-three of her flayed husband's twenty-four vertebrae. But she knows that she won't find the last one, that the last one, she will have to go and ask for it. So that is what she will do, swallowing her pride as queen, she will go and stand before Salina. And when she finds her, in one of the desert refuges where Salina lives surrounded by dried branches and pebbles, she starts by going down on her knees to show Salina she has changed. "The time for forgiveness has come," she says, "don't you feel it, Salina? I do not have long to live but there is still one thing I am waiting for, Salina, before I can bring myself to disappear: Sissoko's last vertebra. If you give it to me, I will go home, I will ask Kano and his men to remove Sissoko's golden stool, I will lay my husband in the ground, I will replace his vertebra and lie down by his side. I will not live one day more. You see, Salina, everything is coming to an end. I have come to ask you for the last vertebra, and if you will give it to me, you will be the victor because, I promise you, I will live no longer." But Salina has stopped listening: her face trembled when old Khaya said Kano's name. She saw herself again as she was in the past, playing those children's games, she saw again the smiling face of the young man they would not let her have. So, when the old woman, still on her knees, has finished talking, when she says these last words in the form of a plea, "Accept, Salina, and we shall both live in our tears," Salina answers and it is to say no. She is not moved by the queen on her knees. She does not offer her hand to help her up. Every word she says is a slap in the face. "You took everything from me, Khaya. Not only my love, but my entire life. You condemned me to the desert. What do I have left, and why should you be able to lie down for eternity with a smile on your lips, you and Sissoko, while I am still damned? Remember that day when I came to find you, to beg you to give me Kano rather than Saro. Remember your arrogance. 'I will knock you senseless with my own hands,' you said. My hatred was born that day, Khaya. And it is my hatred that is replying to you today, because you made it so great that it has traveled with me all through life. It is that long-ago day when you said no that is replying to you now, Khaya. For your man: torment, since I have nothing. For you: the bitter feeling of an unfinished quest. You will be lame, forever. I will let nothing go, Khaya, and the last vertebra will always be missing, because Kano is not mine."

Just as Malaka finishes telling Salina's words, he suddenly stands still. In the distance, for the first time since their departure, the cemetery island is visible. Day is dawning, very pale, placing a new sheen on the surface of the water. The cemetery island is the size of a village, encircled by a high white wall. Around them, the flotilla of boats is even bigger. There must be more than a hundred. He would like to ask if it is like this every time, whenever a man is trying to take his dead to the cemetery, whether this many fishermen accompany the journey, interrupting everything in their lives, living for the time of the crossing on nothing more than the food they exchange with each other, and the stories that are told every night, but he does not dare. He merely observes the armada around them. They are escorting Salina, he thinks, and this moves him. For in her entire life she never saw anything like this: it is like a vast seagoing market, gently rocking.

Just then, some new commotion catches his attention. Visibly, one of the boats is being emptied of its occupants. The adults are handing their belongings onto another boat. The children are also being transferred. Old Darzagar sees Malaka's curiosity and explains.

"They are preparing the boat for the dead woman."

A family of fishermen have offered their boat. This is how it is always done. At a certain point during the crossing, the story of the dead person's life ends up convincing one of the families to make this offering. Without this gift, everything must stop, and the accompanying ferryman must abandon his mission, because no one can hope to enter the cemetery if no living person has offered their boat. For the fishermen who make the offer, it is an honor. If the deceased enters the cemetery, they will be praised, honored, and gain great prestige for their gesture.

"Tonight," Darzagar continues, "we will go a little bit closer and then it will be time to present ourselves at the gate."

The move from one boat to the other is completed. The boat is empty. All along the boat's gunwales, the ferryman arranges dried plants that give off a heady perfume and then, with the assistance of some other men, he carefully transfers Salina's body. Everything has been done now, and calm returns. The men spend the last hours of the day resting and eating, and they finish narrating the dead woman's deed to those who were too far away to hear the story.

"It is time to go closer," says Darzagar, when night has fallen.

And so, the flotilla begins to move, always careful to let Malaka's and Salina's boats go ahead. Malaka knows he can continue with his story, but he doesn't start yet, he waits. He has just seen lights and he is surprised. In the distance, around the island that is slowly coming nearer, fires are burning. He does not ask why. He knows that no one lives there. The cemetery, on its own, has lit up its wall, and it is a splendid sight: a fortress island surrounded by fires glistening on the water, while it waits for people to arrive. Only then does Malaka return to his story.

"I, Malaka, who have come from so far away to bring you my mother, must tell now of the futile passing of time. The hours of idleness and wandering. Salina is nothing now, to anyone. From that day on she began speaking to stones, and haranguing snakes. It dates from that day, the occasional eclipse of her mind that makes her curse the stars. 'Time is passing.' This sentence, such a short one, is a cruel ordeal for those who endure it in solitude. She is far from humanity, and survival exhausts her, she blows on her vengeance to keep it alight because it is all she has left. Time is passing, yes, an entire life, or almost. In the solitude of the desert, all days are alike. Salina crosses the dunes, lets silence go through her. She has changed. Her body is thinner. She has grown used to the heat, has learned the rhythm of the desert. The dew on stones, the white hours of high noon, the cool of evening, and the immense realm of the stars, this is all she knows now. She speaks to no one but herself, and sometimes fights with creatures that covet her meager rations. Time is passing, but for her everything is the same."

And then there comes that day she will long refer to as "the day of the emissary." One evening, at the hour where the heat grows milder, she comes to a well. She knows all the wells, knows, for every one, in which season they are full, and when they are dried up. She goes closer and to her surprise sees a banner planted on the well. There are words printed on it. It takes her some time to decide to go closer. She has not seen a human being in so long that she is not sure she still knows how to speak. Cautiously, she steps forward and finds a young warrior sitting against the well, dozing. He leaps to his feet when he hears her approach.

"What's this?" she asks, pointing to the banner.

He looks at her in amazement—surprised, probably, to see someone appear out of nowhere in such a place. She can sense his fear. He has a weapon, and is wearing the insignia of the Djimba clan, but he is too young to have known the time when she lived among them. Then, from the bag on her shoulder, she takes out some meat which she had dried on the desert stones and offers him some. He accepts and his demeanor becomes milder.

"I am one of the seven emissaries," he says with a knowing air.

When he sees that she does not seem to understand, he explains: for months now, he has been walking through the lands of the North. Kano has given each emissary a region, and nine banners. They all set out with the same mission: plant their nine banners to proclaim the news. Only after they have done this can they return to the kingdom.

"What news?" asks Salina.

"You don't know?"

"I live in the dunes and the dunes have told me nothing."

"King Kano is overjoyed . . . "

"King Kano . . . ?"

He looks at her, astonished, surprised at her ignorance.

"Kano, yes. The son of Sissoko. He became the chief of the Djimba clan when his father died."

"Why do you say he is overjoyed?" she asks.

"Because he has had a son."

She turns pale, would like to speak, but cannot say a word. The emissary continues, "A son. Yes, a long time ago now. That is what I am announcing."

He explains that he and the six other emissaries left on the day of the boy's birth. Each of them had as his mission to go through the region to which he had been assigned in order to spread the news. To plant banners in the farthest regions of the kingdom, in the most inaccessible places so that even there, people, travelers, traders, or remote populations would know that Kano had a son. Then the emissary got lost. He no longer knows how it happened. He left a village further south, then went astray. He no longer knows where he is nor how long he has been away from the world. He has planted his last banner on the well and was beginning to think it would be his grave, so far away from everything does he feel. But Salina is here, she'll be able to help him. She nods. Yes, she knows the way to the villages. He smiles. He will be able to retrace his steps. Perhaps in the meantime Kano has had other children, nothing is impossible . . . but at least he will have carried out his mission.

And then, teeth clenched, trying not to betray her emotion, she dares to ask him her burning question, "And who is the bride?"

The emissary immediately replies, glad to be able to add details to his story, "It is Alika, the daughter of Sal'Elmaya."

Kano proposed this pact between the two clans because the war was never-ending. Sal'Elmaya had invaded the most important trading posts, but the Djimbas, with the help of other desert clans, were engaged in a guerrilla war that prevented Sal'Elmaya from integrating the lands he had conquered. Everyone was exhausted from these battles that no one had the means to win anymore. Kano suggested the alliance, and everyone praised his political wisdom. Trade agreements were sealed. Sal'Elmaya's men withdrew, but they were associated with the taxes levied on the trade from the caravanserais, and the money from spices and cattle.

Salina listens, mute. What could she say? Words are useless, they tear apart her soul, her lips. Has so much time gone by? Another life for Kano. Life as a sovereign, a life of combat, pacts, political motives, and trade agreements. And what has she done? She has wandered from one dune to the next . . .

When the emissary has finished his story, she gets up and walks away, not even saying goodbye to the man she has left behind her.

"Where are you going?" he asks, surprised to see her heading off into the desert where only scarabs and the sun's reflection can live.

"To a place where the news you are bringing has not yet arrived," she answers.

She points him in the direction of the village, due south, then she heads in the opposite direction, into the distance, leaving the emissary behind her and with him all that was said. She goes to the first dune and sits on the summit. She can see everything from there: the well, the banner flapping, the man slowly gathering his belongings then climbing on his animal and riding off. She does not take her eyes off him. He is leaving, going back where he came from, but the banner will stay where it was planted and the words that were said will stay there, too.

IX
THE LAST EXILE

Alone in the dunes, she surrenders. She stays two days without moving, tirelessly repeating the news, trying to understand what is left for her to do. Then, on the third day, she gets up, goes back to the well, and sets off down the road the emissary took when he left. She can sense that it is among people that everything must end. Unless she wants to see Kano again. Or see the face of this woman who shares his bed. Stubborn and staggering at the same time, her face gaunt, she heads toward the Djimba lands so that all may come to an end.

When she reaches the village, after walking for weeks, everything looks the same to her, as if she never left. She finds every bend in the path, every hut, the hills, the first dwellings. She does not realize that no one recognizes her, because she does not realize that the people she sees, these children, the girls bending over the water at the torrent, are so young that they have probably never seen her. To her, everything is the same because she is moving into her past, but people look at her, surprised. It is not common to see a strange woman arrive in their village. The men stop the work they were busy with, the women break off their conversations. She carries on. She does not realize that she no longer looks like a woman. Her skin has hardened in the desert sun. She has something of a hermit about her. She is talking to herself in a low voice, and sometimes she nods to a tree or a rock in greeting. She moves toward the center of the village, does not notice how it has become bigger, how a new opulence cloaks the façades, does not notice that the people she meets are escorting her now, for they have the feeling that she has brought storms with her.

And then finally someone says her name, "Salina!" A woman older than the others has recognized her. And then everything changes. People who were merely curious turn nasty. They have all heard about her. The youngest have been rocked to sleep with stories of those long-ago warriors, Koura Kumba and Mumuyé Djimba, and how the hyenas came, and Khaya's banishment . . . They were told that Salina was the name of misfortune, that Salina was the name of anything that struck the village with the voracity of a cloud of locusts. They have always been taught that Salina is not a name you utter, it is a name you spit. And so that is what they do: they spit, they hound her, they growl behind her back. For the time being, no one has dared to strike her, but that is because they are afraid of her. She continues to walk patiently ahead. The anger around her does not surprise her, nor does it make her tremble. This is what she has come to find: the condemnation of the crowd. She has been vanquished and she knows that the only thing left for the vanquished is to be beaten. As the crowd grows in size, it becomes fiercer, more agitated, surely intoxicated by its own numbers. They mock her, they shove her in the back, surround her so closely that she can feel the joy they take in their cruelty. Some of the women pull her hair. She lets them, and she gets patiently back to her feet when they make her stumble. And finally, they grab her, tie her to a rope, and lead her to the entrance to the village. There, with all the cowardice of those who are great in number, they strut about and slap each other on the back. Then one of them, probably the most cowardly, suggests they tie her to a stake—like a goat, he says, and that makes everyone laugh.

They have put a chain around her neck and fastened it to a pole, and they have left her there at the entrance to the village. Everyone can come and taunt her, insult her, throw fruit peels in her face, spit on her name, or harass her when she sleeps by swatting her legs with thorny branches. Everyone can laugh and feel as if they are burying the old myths. She doesn't move, waits calmly for death, sometimes walks in a circle the way a tired old horse might, drawing a ring of dust on the ground that is the exact depiction of her life.

Until one evening when a woman comes to her. She does not act like the others, does not start insulting her or throwing stones to wake her up with a start. She comes closer, then holds back, cautiously, gazes at her in silence, but does not leave, stays like that, her expression calm and serious. Salina looks at her out of the corner of her eye, grumbles, wonders what she wants, then finally blurts:

"Have you seen what you came to see?"

The woman does not answer. She takes another step forward and, at that moment, enters the circle that, for several days now, has become the territory of Salina's ordeal.

"You want to show me that you're not afraid of me, is that it?" asks Salina, raising her head.

"No," replies the woman calmly, "I want to see what sort of face you have."

"Well then: you've seen me. You can tell the other people around you that you dared to approach the beast . . . You will even be able to tell them that you weren't afraid, that you struck me down with your gaze, you can tell them whatever you like . . . "

"I am Alika," the young woman says then, "the daughter of Sal'Elmaya and the wife of Kano."

Salina freezes, looks at her attentively. Now, suddenly, everything has come to a halt. She was about to turn her back on her, but then she doesn't. She stays there facing the young woman and for the first time she takes a good look at her.

"Alika?" she says again, "the wife of Kano?"

A dark veil passes over her face. She gets to her feet, her expression malicious, and she goes closer, pulling her chain behind her. Alika recoils slightly, but then regains her self-control and remains standing upright.

"You came to see me on the ground?" continues Salina, "you came to make sure Salina is no more than a beast among beasts? You came to see whether what they told you was really true: that the desert had made me old? You came to savor your victory, didn't you? Watch out, Alika. If there is one thing I still know very well how to do, it is how to bleed young ewes."

On finishing her sentence, Salina leaps at her visitor. Young Alika recoils with fear, stumbles, falls backward. Salina laughs with a scornful sneer.

"Go on then, Alika, go and tell your valiant husband

that the woman he once loved is nothing more than a laughing, screaming lunatic. You'll have no trouble convincing him. That is what he wants to hear, more than anything. That I live surrounded by rubbish and spit, and that even the snakes are afraid of me. But don't let that deceive you, Alika: I am what I am because my life was stolen from me. And if blood was spilled, it is because an offense was committed. Go now, Alika, these are old stories that would keep you from sleeping if I told them to you. Go back to your palace."

Alika hears this voice of misfortune, broken, rasping, opening onto worlds of blood and dust, and before she turns her back on Salina, she says simply:

"I came so that no one could say that Alika had not even heard Salina's voice."

"It is not my voice you must hear," says Salina, "because it has been made ugly through hatred. It is my story. But that is not something you have ever done, you never asked to hear it, because otherwise I would know: your ears would have started bleeding long ago."

And the two women part in this way, one going back to the night, and the other resuming her slow walk around the stake, dragging her feet like a mindless animal.

What Alika said to Kano upon her return, no one knows. What she told him about the interview she had just had, no one ever heard. Did she tell him about the pity she felt? Or did she only invoke the terror? Unless she said nothing at all, fearful of opening old wounds. But the morning after the day she went to see Salina, after a long hot day when the village children, once again, played at harassing the old body—insults, mockery, throwing fruit peels, striking her on the legs with branches—on that day when, like the previous ones, hatred has been merrymaking, when evening has begun to fall and calm has returned, it is Kano's turn to go there. He hesitates. When he is standing near the stake, he takes another step, is about to touch Salina, then thinks better of it. She looks at him, remains motionless, says nothing. She immediately recognized him, in spite of the time gone by and their aging faces. She could look at him like that for hours on end. "Let me look at you, Kano . . . " And it is a way of finding the face she had lost, of re-immersing herself for a time in that distant world where she had not yet bled, where Mamambala was alive, that unthreatening world where she could believe that all of life would go by in the gaze of the man she had chosen. "Let me look at you, Kano . . . " She measures the time that has gone by, discovers this stern expression he has, which is new to her, the beard he has, which makes him look old, his bearing, conferred by power. He is in his prime, that age when men have the feeling they are in control of their lives through the choices they make. "Let me look at you, Kano . . . " She knows, Salina does, that life cares little for the will of humans, that life decides in their place, imposes its will, brushes away the paths one would have liked to explore and dissolves what one thought was eternal. She can see, all at once, in this time stretching behind her, what they were and what they are, and she cannot speak, because the words are too far away. So he is the one who speaks, and with the first word he says, she is angry with him, because in the end, it would have been better if they had remained silent, both of them, simply taking the time to gaze at each other one last time, but he

is speaking, that is why he came, and the words are bound
to be petty.

"Why have you come back, Salina?"

She doesn't reply. Is that all he has to say to her? Can
he not, before anything else, make a slow gesture with his
hand to caress her face? Embrace her in silence? Or even
just give her a bit of water out of kindness? Is that the
only question that deserves to be asked?

"So that everything will end, Kano," she replies curtly.

He looks at her. She realizes she is incapable of knowing what he is thinking, what he has inside him, incapable
of saying whether at this moment he is feeling love or disgust.

"Would life not have been sweeter together, Kano?"
she asks hesitantly.

And it is not to try to make him come back to her—she
knows what she looks like, since they chained her to this
stake: a hairy beast, stinking of sweat and exhaustion—it
is just to see if something in him remembers the days of
the past, or simply, perhaps, to erase everything that surrounds them: the dirt, the stake, Alika, the people's cruelty, all of it, and to stay for a time, happy, in the freedom
of their past.

"Why are you asking me this?" he says, coldly.

His reply is like a slap. As if he had indeed used his
hand, but never mind, she tries again.

"Were we not happy, before all this?" And if she asks
the question, it is so that he will come with her along the
paths they took back then, to the streams where they
played in the rainy season, careless of time.

"Before all this . . . " he repeats, his jaw clenched.
"Before the death of my brother, and that of my father?

Before the blood that flowed endlessly on my clan? I don't know anymore, Salina. It's too long ago. 'Before all this' belongs to a world you drowned in blood."

She grits her teeth. Anger is throbbing in her veins. She has tried everything she could, and he is rejecting her, humiliating her. And so, she spits in turn, since that is the only thing left to do.

"But your happiness exists, doesn't it?" she retorts. "Your children, your new power, the confidence you wear on your brow without even noticing, all of that exists and all of that, as you well know, was born of the life I sacrificed. So that you could be happy the way you are today, my own life had to be burned."

"I did nothing, Salina. You blackened yourself with blood all by yourself, through your desire for revenge."

"Did nothing, precisely . . . ever. Not when your brother grabbed me by the hair to make me his, nor when I went to ask your mother for your hand and she spat in my face. You did nothing, when your entire clan exiled me. There was a story, Kano, that you did not fight for."

"You see, Salina, we cannot even speak to one another, cannot even understand each other anymore. There is too much blood between us."

And before she can say anything in reply, he takes a step back, looks at her one last time, and murmurs, "Farewell, Salina," and turns away. She knew it would end like this, she knew the useless words that would do nothing but hurt them, but she would have liked for him to stay a bit longer, for him to stay, even in silence. "Let me look at you, Kano, even if you turn your back on me, let me look at you, because we both know this is the last time."

The hours go by. She would like to die. For it to be all over. Deep down, that is why she came. Why is she living so long? To weep? She has no more tears. To bleed? No blows can hurt her anymore. Life has emptied her, exhausted her. And this is when the hyenas return. In the hours when the village is asleep, the beasts approach. First, there are two of them, then three, then more. At dawn, when the first neighbors walk past Salina's pillory, there are seven of them, lying on the ground, forming a sort of circle. Salina is not moving. She has leaned back against the wooden pole, her head turned toward the sky, and she is murmuring chants, the words inaudible. The children no longer dare throw stones at the prisoner. They are afraid of how the animals might react. "They have come to devour her," say some of the women. "It's almost over," say others. The oldest remember how Salina arrived in the village, and they say she will leave the way she came. They say she should have been left to the hyenas on the very first day, that the animals have come for what is owed them. And yet, not a single animal approaches her. Not a single one tries to bite her. She would not fight them off, she would let them devour her, she's been waiting so long for that. But the hyenas surround her, and it is as if they were protecting her from the people and their rage. Finally, the next day, a group of warriors appears, sent by Kano. The first one stops when he reaches the edge of the circle around the pole, and he speaks loudly to proclaim that, by the will of Kano Djimba, son of Sissoko, Salina will be spared. "In his great wisdom," he says, speaking loudly, "Kano has decided that no more blood must be shed. But so that the dead may not be offended, you have been condemned to exile, Salina. Never again will you be allowed to walk on the lands of the Djimba. Never again will your name be said here." She listens to the guard's words and knows that they are Kano's. She tries to imagine him saying them to her. "By my will, never again, Salina, will you look me in the face. For you, until the end of your days, there will be a walk unto exhaustion." The guards approach slowly, watchful that the hyenas let them pass. They release her, remove her chain, and set her on her feet. She is too weak to stand. They support her, help her take her first steps, and lead her away from the village. "By my will, Salina, never again will these paths hold any trace of you." And thus, the column advances, stumbling. Every time she falls, they pick her up. The hyenas follow, strangely, as if they were tame animals escorting the small group. Only once they have reached the edges of the kingdom do they move away and disappear, as if they had just wanted to make sure the men would not hurt Salina. When they reach the edge of the Djimba lands, the warriors take their long spears and, poking her gently in the back or on her calves, they oblige Salina to move ahead on her own, until she has passed the outermost bounds of the kingdom, and they make sure she does not retrace her steps. "By my will, never again, Salina . . . " And so, she keeps on, regains the strength to walk, slowly, and enters her third exile.

Everything should have ended like that, with her figure disappearing into the desert. Salina walking unto exhaustion, then dying, then drying out until she became a little sun-bleached pile of bones, a landmark for the hyenas in the vast expanse of their hunting. But a rider is following her. She does not realize right away, does not turn around, keeps going straight ahead, to the slow rhythm of her exhaustion. On the second day of her drifting, the rider catches up with her, overtakes her, and dismounts. Salina looks up. She has gone too far into her weariness to find the strength to be surprised. She simply looks at the rider and tries to understand what she is doing here. The rider is a woman. It takes Salina a while to recognize her. She searches in her dazed mind for where she has seen her, but she cannot place her. The woman sees this and says her name, "I am Alika, daughter of Sal'Elmaya and wife of Kano." She removes the cloth covering her hair, protecting her from the sun. She takes out a leather gourd which she hands to Salina so she may drink. Salina's movements are slow. She cools her throat. Then Alika begins to speak.

"What I must do, Salina, no woman before me has ever done." She speaks and her voice betrays an emotion she has felt since she left the village. "This day will always be that of my great loss. But I must do it, I know I must . . . "

Salina is listening now and there is a new spark in her eyes.

"I demanded that Kano tell me your story, Salina. I never interrupted him, other than to ask him for more details when it seemed to me that he was going too quickly. Yes, you have lost. Your body shows it now, worn and wrinkled. You have been humiliated. There is nothing left for you, I know that. I ought to be glad. For the Djimbas are on the side of the victors and I am one of them. They all smile when someone says your name because they know they have nothing left to fear from you, but they are wrong. I know that a war is only ever truly over when the victor agrees to lose in turn. That is why I have come, Salina."

She pauses. Salina says nothing, does not understand what is about to happen. The young woman delicately removes an infant from under her long shawls. She holds it in the curve of her arm.

"This is my last-born child, Salina. The son of a loving mother. But I have brought him to you because there must be a gift between the Djimbas and Salina. Only in this way can everything come to an end. I am here to give you my son. You will take him. You will watch over him, you will raise him like a mother. Take him, Salina. I will be severed from him forever. As will Kano. Not a day will go by that we will not think of him, and of you, and that is as it should be. Because then there will be no arrogance on either side, but an equal mixture of smiles and tears. Take him, Salina, take him because I can tell, in this final moment, that I do not quite have the strength to tear him from my arms. I have not given him a name, you will do that. Take him, Salina, and remember Alika's gift."

Salina slowly reaches out, delicately takes hold of the cloth in which the child is wrapped, feels his weight in the curve of her arms, and smiles. Instinctively, she holds him close, and she weeps, in a way she has not wept for a whole lifetime. Then, hesitantly, she unclasps a necklace she was wearing beneath her rags of dust and hands it to the young woman.

"I have only this to offer you in exchange, Alika: this, which is nothing in comparison to the child you are giving me. But in this way, the blood of the past will be buried. For you, Sissoko's last vertebra. Let peace return. As I hand it to you, it all seems long ago and unbelievable.

Forgive me. I am taking the life you are giving me. I will watch over your son—for he will always be your son, Alika. When he grows up, it is your features I will see on his face and that will be good. Before my eyes I will have the face of your wisdom. Go, Alika: what you have done, no mother has ever done. I will live, I swear to you. Do not worry about my ruined body and my exhaustion. I wanted to die, but now everything has changed. The desert will be my kingdom. I will teach him everything I know. He will have the stars for a godfather and the hyenas for his retinue. He will grow tall and handsome. I swear it. Go, Alika, I will take him, this son you are giving me, and I will tell him what you did, the strength you had, I will keep nothing from him, so that he will know that he is the child of two mothers and of a consecrated peace, the child who has buried the old blood. I will tell him that Alika is the name of the gift. And he will live, open and just, wherever he goes."

Alika, gently, climbs back on her mount and, trying to silence the sobs that have gripped her, slowly goes back the way she came. Salina watches her disappear and allows a life she thought had vanished to well up inside her. In that moment, she knows that something has begun. An existence for two, where she will have to teach, and feed, and protect; a life, at last.

X
THE RESPONSE OF THE CEMETERY

Malaka interrupts his story and looks all around. The cluster of boats is motionless. The cemetery island lies a few hundred yards ahead.

"It is time to go up to the gate," says the ferryman, and he gives a sudden thrust of his oar so that his boat and Salina's move away from the flotilla. Malaka stares apprehensively at the surrounding wall.

"What will you do if the gate opens?" he asks.

"My destiny is to accompany the body of your mother to the end," the old man replies simply.

Everything is slow and calm. The two boats move at equal speed toward the island. Malaka knows the ferryman's efforts alone could not have been enough to bring them this far. He also knows that, on this night, he must not try to understand everything with his mind. The boats move forward because the cemetery is calling them. After a while, when they are very near, the doors of the gate begin to move. Malaka holds his breath, hoping with all his being . . . Yes, the gate is opening. The cemetery will accept Salina, the woman of three exiles, the woman who had one hated son, one anger son, and one son to redeem everything, Salina, the woman turned to salt by her tears, condemned to be born and to die walking through unknown lands. The cemetery island has accepted her. A smile crosses Darzagar's face. Slowly, he gets up and, before Malaka has time to ask him what he is doing, he moves nimbly onto the dead woman's boat. Once he is on board, he sits in the stern, then looks one last time at Malaka and murmurs:

"You have brought the story of your mother to us; it is time to let go of it now. It is up to others to take it and tell it. Henceforth, it will be on our lips. The city has adopted it. You can live. The time for you to carry your legacy is ending. It's your turn to be part of the world. Everything lies ahead. Others, one day, will tell the story of who you were. Go, Malaka, you know it well, you felt it the moment you were finishing your story: everything comes to an end and everything begins at the same time."

And then he turns away, settles on the seat as if he were going to row, but he does not move, he sits very straight, watching over the body with the silence of a statue. The two boats drift apart. Darzagar moves away with Salina's body at his feet. The sea is calm. The gate to the cemetery is wide open now. There are lights inside and a vast network of canals irrigates the island like a labyrinth of water interlaced with marble. The boat moves through the threshold of the gate and is about to penetrate further in. No sooner has it entered the enclosure than the two doors begin to close slowly behind it. Malaka does not move. He wants to see her until the end. The boat goes a bit further, then disappears while the doors finish closing. For Salina, rest at last. For Salina, an entire city that accepts her, at last. Malaka weeps, unburdened of this long life, which has now stopped here in this strange darkness, about to turn rosy with the first rays of daylight. He is weeping, the son of the mother with her name like salt. All around him, the fishermen have begun to sing, drumming on tablas, and playing unfamiliar instruments to celebrate this holy day when the cemetery reopened its gates. He weeps as he thinks of who he is: the son with two mothers, the gift child. And Alika's name comes to his lips. In this moment of saying goodbye to Salina, it is only right that he say Alika's name, so the two will be side by side in this hour of endings. He closes his eyes, and, in his mind, he embraces them. When he opens his eyes again, every boat, as a sign of joy, has lit a fire at its prow, and Malaka sees an endless garland of torches rocking gently around him. He knows that, in a few minutes, the boats will start to move apart from each other. They will scatter like a huge crowd. They will go back to their lives, taking Salina's story with them. She is one of them, now. He is calm. He knows he will never be the same. Darzagar told the truth: in these moments when everything is ending, the days to come are being born, and he is ready. And so, before heading back to the shore to melt once again into the world, to be a man among others and build his own life, he stays a brief while longer looking at the cemetery, with the cluster of boats behind him, and he murmurs, "Farewell, Salina," then smiles, glad that, for a time, he was the storyteller.